My Life with a Criminal: Milly's Story
an exciting sequel to the best-selling novel
My Life in Crime by John Kiriamiti

When, as an innocent teenage girl, Miriam met John Kiriamiti, alias Jack Zollo, she found him gentle, kind and considerate. She fell into a passionate romantic love with this man who claimed to be a car salesman, and who continued to present the image of the perfect gentleman — for months, running into years, never abusing her trust and for this long period continuing to respect her virtue and her virginity.

But finally, with a clean conscience and with the blessing of her own mother , she moved in with this man she loved. And that is when she began to notice that her lover had a double life. It started with the realization that this man never had an office ... he operated from a noisy bar.... Then there were the little, heavy, sharp-pointed, dull-golden objects hidden in a chalk-box ... and, one day when she came home early from the office, the stumbling on five men in her sitting room conspiratorially sharing out bank notes.

Her discovery of her man's double life did not constrain her to run away from him, for her love was the love of a life time. But her life and love started to exact a heavy price: she constantly walked the tightrope of stress as she sat out nights waiting for a man who at such moments was involved in gun fights and car chases with the police. Could she ever hope of settling down with this man, of consummating the love that had consumed her being?

Milly was Jack Zollo's (alias John Kiriamiti's) girlfriend and her story is told, from the criminal's point of view, in an earlier book, *My Life in Crime*. This is now Milly's poignant story about her life with the bank robber.

SPEAR BOOKS SERIES

My Life with a Criminal
Milly's Story

a sequel to
John Kiriamiti's best selling novel
My Life in Crime

Spear Books
NAIROBI, KAMPALA

Published by Spear Books
a subsidiary of
East African Educational Publishers Ltd.
Brick Court, Mpaka Road/Woodvale Grove
Westlands
P.O. Box 45314
Nairobi

East African Educational Publishers Ltd.
Pioneer House, Jinja Road
P.O. Box 11542
Kampala

First published 1989
Reprinted 1989 (twice), 1990 (twice),
1991, 1993, 1995, 1996

ISBN 9966-46-768-8

Printed in Kenya by FotoForm Ltd.
Muthithi House, Westlands
P.O.Box 14681, Nairobi.

Chapter 1

Call me Milly, because he made you believe I liked the name. He never once told you that I had begged him hundreds of times not to make the name stick. I was born with a touch of Christianity and I didn't like shortcuts, especially when it came to names.

My mom called me Nyambiu when she bore me. The Catholic Father she took me to, soon after, called me Miriam, which was confirmed by a Bishop sometimes later; then the man I so loved nicknamed me Milly and refused to listen to my appeals against it. He made me feel like a criminal — I guess he was a confirmed one himself, with more nicknames than he ever let you know. Yes, he was my man; a man whose love no woman could resist; a man you'd think you knew all about, while you actually knew nothing.

I didn't know my dad, until I was eleven, when my mom pointed out a man and said he was the one. She had to; I had become too alert to the number of men coming in and out of her room for her to ignore it much longer.

In the days when he was living with us, dad was a terrible drunkard. He only came home drunk to claim for food violently — food he hadn't bought. He used to sleep out so often that it became difficult to know whether he had spent the night in a police cell, in a lodging with a hag or out in the cold in a drunken stupor.

Believe me, none of this ever bothered my dad, not even the fact that our door often remained unlocked throughout the night, so that he would have easy entry at whatever hour he came home.

When I was about five years old, my mother couldn't

1

tolerate my dad any longer. He had become a burden. She decided to call it quits with this 'symbol' of a husband and try life on her own. She took my younger sister, Cathleen Mumbi, and I to her sister's place in Eastleigh and left us there.

Life with my aunt, Damaris Nyakio, was lovely. She was married to a businessman — uncle Wanjau — who was very nice and polite. She treated us like her own children and since mom came to see us often, we really never missed her for the one year we stayed at Eastleigh.

In December 1958, mom came for us and took us to Bahati, where she had found a bedsitter, which we all shared. She also sent me to a school, just opposite our new home.

Now that she was single, mom paid the house rent all by herself. Even though when dad used to live with us he was supposed to meet the rent, we were often embarrassed when he refused to and the landlord would throw us out. We missed dad at times; my sister for one could not go for a week without mentioning him. But as the years went by we got used to being without him. It was good riddance, I guess.

He came back to visit us when I was in standard four. By then mom had started selling beer at our home, and I didn't blame her for we had to survive, somehow. Whenever dad was drunk he would wage war on other customers and almost chase them away. He would at times refuse to leave and spend the whole night on the sofa disturbing our peace. I hated him then. I hated married life and I have hated men in general, ever since.

Somehow he found out that he wasn't welcome in our home and gave up coming. One year later we got news that he had married his neighbour's housemaid, who then left him after her second delivery.

Life in Bahati wasn't bad at all, especially for me, for I never once stayed idle. When I had finished helping my mom with the housework, I would go straight to the books. There was nothing I liked better than studying, and teaching my sister. I had no time at all to play with other children. When my sister was not around, I kept to myself. Although my mom never once took us to church, as she never went herself, I introduced myself to one just a few metres from our home and I never failed to attend. At times I think I was a born Christian. My life was honest; I loved my mom; I loved my dad, but hated his sinful life; I loved my neighbours and everything that God had granted me. I also loved the vicinity in which God had decided I would live and grow up, but I hated sinning, more than I hated sitting on a snake. I was glad that my mom realised what type of a daughter she had and helped me to remain clean.

I was growing up rapidly and by the time I had completed primary education, I was almost my mom's size in height. Her beer-selling business was now big. At times, patrons would come in great numbers, until she would be forced to request some to take their beer outdoors. Some would get too drunk and almost mistake me for her, trying to make passes at me. Mom never minded being touched on the breasts, even by young men; but accidental touch like that on me would make me go for nights without sleep. I so loathed it with all my heart that the thought of such a thing happening to me would make me go crazy. Thank goodness my mom saw what was happening and did the most admirable thing. She rented another room next to her bar, for me and my sister, and one whom I no doubt

3

knew was on the way. I wasn't so naive as to fail to notice that my mom was pregnant.

I did the Kenya Preliminary Examination and passed well. That was given, anyway, I couldn't fail. Unfortunately I was called to Kenya High School, even though it wasn't amongst any of my choices. The problem was that my mother could not afford the school fees, which was very high. So, through the help of some of her patrons who knew more than one thing, I got a place in Ngara Girls' High School.

Once in the secondary school, my life became different. I now got up earlier than usual and prepared breakfast for the whole family. As my sister was also in school, I would see her off before I took a bus to town and then change to another one for Ngara. My mother, who had started other business in town, usually left before 6 a.m.

I became social and made friends with girls of my own age at school. Often we would go out for lunch together. At times some of my friends would be picked by boys to go for lunch and would request me to join them. Even though I didn't want a boyfriend of my own, I didn't mind being with them and, as long as they didn't misbehave, I enjoyed every moment when we went out together.

Everything was going on well at home. My mom's businesses were paying well and we could afford to meet our needs. Mom was living to keep us happy and well provided for. I for one got whatever I desired, because in me she saw a great future. By the time I was completing the second year in secondary school, the baby boy my mother had begot was big enough to be left behind while she went out. We decided to employ a maid and from then on my housework became lighter and I got more opportunities to study. The following year I enrolled at Bahati Social

Hall for typing classes in the evenings.

By now my friends in school had started wondering what I was made of. Although I continued going out with their so-called boyfriends, I never engaged myself with any and they too never saw any approaching me. Sometimes I even paid for the meals we took with their boys and this perplexed them. They decided to cross-examine me. One day I went out for lunch with my three best girlfriends. Wanja, who was our class prefect started it all:

"Miriam...", she hesitated shyly, "tell us, have you ever been laid?"

"I was born, I wasn't laid, are you mad, Penny?" In fact I hadn't got her meaning. I had taken her question literally. I sensed I was wrong when the rest burst out in peals of laughter.

"Why don't you ask her a direct question, Penny?" Njambi said, when she had cut short her loud laughter. By then I already had got what she was driving at. I was quiet, rather annoyed.

"Milly, have you ever had a boyfriend in your life?"

"No, and I do not think I'll ever have; it isn't necessary."

"Do you know what you are missing, dear?" asked Penny.

"Boys are very sweet Milly. Just try one," added Amina.

"Penny, how can you miss something you do not know? What do you see in men, and what is that sweet thing in them, Amina?" I asked

"I'll tell my boyfriend, Joe, to come with his friend next time. He will befriend you and you'll find out the rest for yourself", said Njambi.

"Let him not waste his calories for nothing. Why don't you have the two of them yourself?"

"I'd lose both of them and I cannot do without my Joe. Can you do without a boyfriend Penny?"

5

"I wouldn't get any sleep if I lost mine," said Penny. "I wouldn't get any sleep if I dreamt of having a boyfriend," I said, and I meant it.

I was relieved when the bell rang. This teasing, I knew, could continue for days, probably weeks, but I didn't mind. I forgot the whole thing each time I got home and went straight to my typing lessons, then to private studies. But before men gave up on me, I had to turn down hundreds. I just could not bring myself to entertain a man and give him my precious time. No, not me!

There is this Wednesday I'll never forget. It was March 12, and I was in my final year in secondary school. The previous night I hadn't slept well. I felt sick and could not even concentrate on my studies, which worried me. I woke up late the following morning, as I hadn't been able to fall asleep until 5.00 a.m. In a hurry, I prepared myself for school, picked up my bag and dashed out of the room. My mom's voice stopped me in my tracks:"Nyambiu!"

"Yes, Mom." I went back to know what she wanted.

"What is the matter with you this morning? You woke up late, did your work in a hurry and even before you have taken breakfast, you dash out like a mad girl." I laughed because I knew she was only joking. She knew I was obedient and I knew she was proud of me.

"Did you take your busfare and money for lunch, do you have some with you?"

"I had forgotten mom, I hate being late." Though I took it lightly I was surprised that I should forget. I took the money and went out. I got a bus in good time. The conductor, seeing I was a school girl asked for my pass. "Yes, I have one," I answered. I looked for it in my school bag, but it wasn't there. Yet I was sure I had put it in. I must

6

have lost it and so I prepared myself to pay the adult fare. But the conductor understood and charged me half-fare. It is easy to dismiss this minor bus-pass incident but, somehow, it has haunted my life ever since. By lunchtime, my mood was back to normal and I joined my friends as usual. Some distance from the gate, we noticed a young handsome and smartly dressed man. To me, he was just that: smart. But not so with the others. Amina, who liked joking more than she liked her food, addressed me: "Milly, wouldn't you like a beauty like that one?"

We all laughed at the joke. But as we approached the gate, I noticed that the young man was staring at me. The nearer we got to him, the surer I became that his eyes were focussed on me and I became frightened. Then as we reached where he was, he called my name!

My friends broke out in laughter and I became so confused that I didn't know how to react. Should I stop and talk to him or not? Then all of a sudden it struck me: he was not just a boy like my friends were used to. He was handsome and smartly dressed and certainly no comparison to the boys we were used to. This one, even to my friends, was a beauty.

"Yes, hallo. How are you?" I called.

"Quite okay, and you?" he answered.

"Just the same," I said and shrugged. Then he insisted on introductions, which we carried out.

On that day, I met Jack Zollo. He had brought me my bus-pass, which I had dropped on the way to the bus-stop that morning.

Even though my friends always insisted that I accompany them and their boyfriends for lunch, when Jack invited me, I felt reluctant to ask them along. I wanted him all to myself. Strangely, I felt attracted to him and I didn't want to share his lunch with my friends. He was the only man I had ever admired, so far and I wanted to be close to him.

We walked to a restaurant nearby and took seats. I couldn't believe what was happening to me. Was this really me seated with a man in a restaurant? And not just a man, but a total stranger? Why did I feel attracted to him? What did he think of me when I accepted his offer without a flinch of the eye? And who was he? Would he dismiss me, after handing over the bus-pass, after the lunch? No he wouldn't. But what would he think of me if I told him that he was the first man I had ever sat down with? Would he believe me if I told him I was a virgin? Would he just laugh and dismiss it as a joke or mere imagination?

Even as all these questions were going through my mind, I knew that my life had changed. Jack Zollo had walked into my life and unknowingly changed it completely. I wondered if he was aware of the effect he had on me; an effect even I couldn't understand.

After lunch, he escorted me back to school. We talked and exchanged contacts. I learnt that he worked for DT Dobies as a salesman. I told him where I lived and hoped that he would ask me out for a date. I longed to see him smile, to hear him say that he had fallen in love with me, or just that he liked me and would want to see me again. But my boy did none of these things. He begrudged me even the smile, which I thought was the sweetest I have ever seen. I had to content myself with stealing side glances at him, and oh my, what a man!

We stopped at the gate and I found myself shaking at the thought of seeing him go. I knew he didn't know what was happening to me, and if he did, then he was a good actor for he certainly didn't show it. My friends came along and stopped to say hello. I introduced them, and as each shook his hand, I couldn't help but be jealous, and wish that they would hurry and leave us alone, for they were shaking hands with *my* boy. My boy he was, whether he knew it or not.

The school bell rang, reminding us that classes were just five minutes away. My friends bade my boy goodbye and they left me stranded. Should I ask him to meet me in the evening so that we would go home together? What would he think of me if I did that — wouldn't he think that I was too eager or cheap and easy to come by? Oh! Why couldn't women have an outward sign, declaring them virgins, when they were? It would be so easy, so convenient. Then no man would mistake us for what we are not and things would be so much simpler.

But none of my wishful thinkings helped, for I couldn't bring myself to give a man a date. Finally, I stretched out my hand to say goodbye and he took it. The touch of his hand sent a chill down my spine. Then he did it: he squeezed my fingers and I almost went down, for my knees became too weak to support me. It was so warm and throbbing all over that I wished the moment would never pass. Then, for the first time in a long time, he smiled at me:

"When do I see you again Milly?" And Milly I became.

"Any time you feel like," I stammered.

"I'll come to take you out for lunch tomorrow. Is it okay with you?"

"Quite okay. Please do. P-l-e-a-s-e. I have to run to class now." Upon which I disengaged myself, reluctantly though, and ran off to class.

Back in class, I was glad I had met this man. I sat for the last two papers of the monthly examination and scored top marks, jumping far ahead of my classmates. That boyfriend of mine had motivated my brains.

On the way home with my friends, my thoughts were on Jack. I longed for his company, which reminded me of the incident when my friend Penny had said that she couldn't do without her boyfriend. It made me wonder whether I too had now reached a point where I couldn't do without Jack, just one day after meeting him.

Jack Zollo. What a nice name, I thought to myself.

"You sure have a nice piece, Miriam. What does he do?" asked one of the girls on our way home that evening.

"He is a salesman with DT Dobie. Believe me, Njambi, I met him today and I feel he has been mine all along." I couldn't believe that I had said that.

"But he is nice. I quite liked him, although he looks too innocent and talked with a smooth voice. That one will give you a very nice time," Penny, the expert, contributed. I wished I could believe her.

At home, everyone noticed and commented on my extraordinary happy mood. I didn't volunteer any information, but I was glad that they had noticed the change in me. That night, I dreamt that I was in bed with him, on his huge king-size bed. I was telling him what I felt about him when I felt someone shaking me violently. I woke up to the protests of my sister who was claiming that I was disturbing her sleep. Before my temper got the better of me, I reasoned that I must have been dreaming loudly, and so left her alone. But I didn't go back to sleep after that. The rest of the night was spent in imagining him waiting for me at the school gate. The night was so long, it seemed like a week to me.

He came to take me out for lunch the following day, as promised. Again, I did not invite my girlfriends along,

10

and this, I argued, was due to my natural jealousy, for I did not want them to share the company of my boy; I did not want them to feel the tender touch of those small hands of my Jack, or him to smile at them. He was mine — all mine, and I did not see why I should share him with anyone else.

His many surprises started on that day. We crossed the road and he led me to a nearby parking lot. I had no idea where we were going, but judging from the way he was dressed and where he worked, I knew he'd be out of place in the fish and chips places my friends and I frequented. I saw him take out a bunch of keys and select one. He went to a Datsun and unlocked it. Seconds later he opened the passenger door for me and for the first time in my life, I entered a car which I had good reason to believe was part of my life.

We drove towards town, and the boy could drive. I liked the way he overtook other cars, and I knew he was driving fast so that he could get me back to school on time. We didn't stop in town. On reaching University Way he turned right and entered Harry Thuku road. We passed Norfok Hotel and the VOK and went on to Hotel Boulevard. It was the first time for me to be in a hotel of this class. Most of the patrons here were white, and that answered at least a question or two I had about my boy. When the bill came I was surprised. In the hotels that we frequented with my friends and their boyfriends, the seven of us would spend twenty shillings and get some change back. Out of the hundred shillings note Jack gave to the waiter, he received change of about seven shillings, which he did not even take, explaining that it was something called a "tip" in those big hotels.

Well, I didn't like this man for his money, or because

he worked with DT Dobie, or whatever else it was that made him what he was. I liked him because I believed he was made for me.

"Do you drink? I mean do you take beer?" I asked him on our way back to school.

"Yes, why? Don't you like people who drink?"

"I am sorry. I just wanted to tell you mom sells beer at home." I wanted to invite him home but I didn't have the guts to. On the other hand he could not come to my room, because mom wouldn't allow it. But if he knew home, he might just pay us a visit.

"So if I happen to come, what happens? Will you buy me beer or smuggle a bottle or two to where I'll be hiding?" Well, he had started talking the way I wanted him to. He had a sense of humour.

"Oh no, I just can't afford to buy beer. But can't you just sit with the rest in the room?"

"Will you be serving me?

"I am sorry again, mom will not let me in the room with customers."

"You stay out until the last customer goes away?" He was sympathetic, almost annoyed. I detected much concern in his voice and this made my heartbeats louder.

"Oh no, she has rented a room for me, next to hers." I saw relief cross his face as he sighed with satisfaction.

"Thaz bearifu. I like it."

"Thank you."

"Why?"

"I . . . I . . . don't know . . . I mean . . . it is . . ." I stammered. In fact I did not know why I was thanking him. The way he looked at me as I stammered for an answer sent a chill down my spine.

"So what next? Here we are." We had arrived at the

12

school gate, and in good time too, but I could see he wanted to go. I was confused and did not know what to say.

"I'll come home this evening, if you promise to buy me beer. Will you?"

"Please do. I'll buy for you what I can afford."

He dipped his hand into his pocket and took out a hundred shilling note. I was shocked. That kind of money was too much for me. In fact, it needed only another twenty shillings to pay our house rent for two months. I heard myself saying, "Please no, please don't; I don't need it. You need it, Jack, but not me. What would I do with all that money?"

He smiled as he put it back; I think he understood how overwhelmed I was. He took out a twenty shilling note and I accepted it, not because I needed it, but because I did not want to disappoint him.

"Bye till then." He gave me his hand and when I took it, he squeezed my fingers the same way he had done the previous day. I felt owned.

Amina and Njambi were waiting for me outside our classroom, when I arrived, and before anything else we were on it: discussing our boyfriends. Mine, of course, was the main topic.

"That one will drive you nuts. And he is so young that that car can't be his. It must be his father's."

"It is a company car, but he looks like he owns one himself?" I said.

"Imagine going out in a car and you can't even invite us, you can't be so mean."

"You've got to understand that this man is very new to me and if I..."

"Sorry, I wasn't serious, Miriam. I was just making fun." I felt ashamed. I guess, I was too jealous to want to share

13

my boy with my friends. But I couldn't help it, and hoped that they would eventually understand and forgive me.

While waiting to change buses that evening in town, I passed by a telephone booth and remembered the numbers Jack had given me. I looked at my watch and saw it was before four o'clock. I guessed Jack must still have been in the office and decided to call him. The booth was empty, so I entered. The answer came almost on the first ring.

"Hello, can I help you?"

It was a man's voice.

"Can I speak to Jack Zollo, please?"

He kept silent for a while. I didn't know whether I was imagining it or not, but I could hear music coming clearly on the phone, and I wondered whether I had called a wrong number. But then I heard the same voice call me back.

"Ngojea, anaitwa kutoka huko juu."

I waited for two minutes then I heard his soft voice.

"Hello, Zollo speaking." The music could be heard distantly.

"How are you, I decided to call you before going home."

"And who are you?" I guess I detected some harshness in his voice this time and I almost doubted it was him.

"This is Miriam; don't tell me you cannot recognize my voice." I head a relief in his breath.

"Ooh . . . it is you dear!" It was the first time for him to call me "dear" and I almost jumped with joy. "Where are you calling from?"

"I am in town, on my way home; I came by a telephone booth and decided to try and see if I could get you in the office."

"Do you want any help? I can come and rush you home."

"No, thank you. I only felt I should speak to you."

14

"It is okay, the promise is still intact. I'll come."

"Thank you, do you play music in the office? I hear lots of it."

"You are imagining it, probably. But, this is a mad office. How is everything?"

"Quite okay." I answered, then wondered what things he was referring to and about which I said *okay*.

"You have a nice voice, Milly, I like it. It makes me love you." My heart started racing. No man had ever said that to me. Not that I wasn't lovable, but I had never given anyone the chance to say it before. It sounded very sweet coming from this particular man; it is what I had been longing for over the last two days.

"Do you?"

"Do I what?" Should I mention it?, I asked myself. I felt shy, but since he couldn't see me, nor challenge me with those eyes of his, I said: "Love me?"

"Well . . . I don't know. Can one really love you enough?" What did he mean? Could he probably have been taking me for a child, because I was a school girl or did I look like one? Could he have found out somehow that I was a virgin and probably thought that I could not do what he might suggest? Would this make him leave me? I started getting worried. "God help me" I prayed in the booth.

"Milly, are you still there?"

"Yes, I am." I felt like weeping.

"And why go to silence so abruptly?"

"You asked me a very hard question."

"Which one?"

"Whether one can really love me enough. Am I too young for love?"

"No, dear, not that. I mean you are too good to be push

15

ed about with mere words. One needs to be near you to
answer that question."

"Do I mean that much to you?"

"More than you can guess, I wish I could get you away
from everyone else."

"What would you do?"

"Everything on this earth. I could even eat you alive."

"Jack, are you drunk? I can't believe you are not."

"Then I am very sorry, excuse my haste, I am sorry."

"Please do not say that, you haven't wronged me."

"I see I love you."

"Thank you."

"For?"

"Loving me. I just can't believe it. Why didn't you tell
me before?"

"When and where Milly? Why do you think I took all
the trouble of bringing the bus-pass to you?"

"Why did you bring it? Just tell me, please."

"The picture on it was beautiful. I wanted to see what
the original looked like. If it had one eye I'd have thrown
it in the nearest dustbin."

"And how was the original compared to the picture?"

"No comparison, dear absolutely no comparison, not
even to the others in the school."

"I am glad you think that, Jack."

"No, not thinking, I am sure, and let me tell you Milly,
you are the first girl I have ever loved . . . I hardly do it."

I went home very happy. I could not believe I had been
talking to Zollo.

I was waiting outside the house when he came. There
were about seven customers and my mom wasn't in.
Although I was left in charge of the little beer that remain-

ed when she went for more, I was not to enter the room.
My duty was to open the room where the drinks were and
one of her regular customers did the selling. But now that
my boy had come, I couldn't stay out; I felt protected.

Jack was the first and only person I served. Every time
I looked at him, the telephone conversation came flowing
back into my mind. I couldn't believe that this was the same
person I had talked with. I couldn't imagine the sweet words
coming from him and that he was now here.

He was on his fourth beer when mom returned with ad-
ditional stock. On entering the room I was surprised to see
that she went straight to Jack and shook hands with him.

"I am mama Nyambiu," she told him, still gripping his
hand. Smiling, he told her:

"I am Jack Zollo."

"Thank you, you are welcome here."

Mom then turned to me and asked. "Are you selling today? You are becoming a nice girl."

She looked at me, then at Jack, and whatever she
thought, she was right. She had never seen me in the room
with the drinkers. Nor had she seen a young man of Jack's
class in that home before, which made all this more than
a mere coincidence. But I didn't want her to confirm her
suspicions. It could hurt her to think that I was about to
leave her.

Back in my room, I could hardly concentrate on
anything. My boyfriend was only six metres away and I
couldn't be with him. I would leave whatever I was doing
and go to the room, pretending that I had left one thing
or another there. A glance at him would satisfy me and
I'd go back to my room. Ten minutes later I would
remember another thing I had left there and I'd go back
to look for it, taking five long minutes before I "found"

17

it. I finally gave up when mom asked: "Did you leave almost everything you had here? You've come here five times in thirty minutes."

She didn't intend to hurt me but merely to let me know that she wasn't fooled by immature tricks. I respected her; I loved her as much as I loved myself and anything she said to me was acceptable, because I knew that the last thing she would do was to hurt my feelings. Knowing that my tricks had come to an end and that I would not get a chance to talk to Jack, I went back to my room and took a pen and a piece of paper. I wanted him to go with me in his heart. The following day was a Saturday and since I wouldn't go to school, I knew I couldn't wait till Monday, when he probably would think of coming to see me, and so I wrote a note:

My Dear Jack,

> *I knew this would happen. Although we didn't get time to talk, I hope you understand that I wanted to see you and you knew where I live. We must not show mom what is going on between us. Please know that I am for you, wherever you are. I cannot wait until Monday to see you. On Sundays I go to a church of my choice. I want to see you then. Could you please meet me in town, at St. Peter's Clavers, on Race Course Road, at around 9.30 a.m.! Please, Jack, don't fail to come; I must see you.*

> *Yours forever,*
> *M.N.*

"Miriam."

I turned. It was my younger sister.

"Aren't you teaching me English today? You told me yesterday that today we would learn English."

Well, I did not know how to explain why I couldn't keep the promise. Instead of keeping my promise to her, I had had to make sure I saw Jack as he left so that I could give him the letter. After that my sister could have my attention.

Jack received the note without a problem; it was as if he expected it. He took it and put it in his pocket, wished me goodbye and left immediately. I went back to my room to keep my promise to my sister, Mumbi. This time she would have all my attention.

On Sunday I woke up earlier than usual, for I wanted to be in time for my date with Jack. I had spent the Saturday at my aunt's place, bored almost to death, a thing that had never happened in my life before. I was restless and surprised her by announcing that we would go home early. My sister, however, overruled me, to my aunt's joy, and I spent the afternoon in silence, with Jack dominating my mind.

I waited for almost two hours outside the church until the first mass ended. He still hadn't come, so I went in for the second mass. But I was so preoccupied with thoughts about him that for the first time since I started going to church, I did not receive the body of Christ.

Eight months after I met Jack, I sat for my 'O' levels. They had been eight months of heavenly bliss, the experience of a lifetime.

A month before the examinations, he sent me a success card that made my heart go raving crazy. It was beautiful and expensive, and carried the best message I had ever read: ". . .*It is only your best performance that will tell me I never interfered with your school life. Only that alone will erase the guilty conscience in me. My fate depends on your performance. . .*"

It hadn't occured to him that since I met him I had improved my performance at school greatly.

It took us almost one month to complete the examinations. Every morning I would meet him, waiting for me at the bus-stop. In most cases he would have a car, a different one each day. On two occasions we rode in a taxi. He would come to take me out for lunch and drop me home in the evening. Sometimes he would take some beer at home and then go away. We were careful not to worry mom, so we did it secretly. On one occasion I had to bend down in the car and cover myself with the school sweater, when Jack spotted her at the bus-stop on our way. But she was busy talking with her friend and couldn't see us.

I was lucky that during all the time I was in school, Jack never asked me to go to bed with him. He believed that it would interfere with my education, which I doubted. "Milly," he told me one day, "you are still naive in this mad world. Just do what I ask of you and you'll never regret." He already knew that I was a virgin and had decided to treat me in his own way.

Before the examination results were out, I had completed my typing course and as I waited for the results, I got a job with East African Airways. I was now 18 years old. We could now meet more often, with fewer risks of mom finding out. I hated the thought of offending her, but comforted myself by saying that up to that time, I hadn't done anything I could be ashamed of. And I gave the credit to Jack.

The new year found us eagerly waiting for the results,

but with different reasons. I was eager to surprise him, because I knew I had done well, and he was eager to know how I had fared. The day the results came out, I called him. I could still hear music in the background and this time it took about five minutes before he came on the line.

"Hello, is that Jack?"

"At his best," he answered. He had, I guessed, recognized my voice.

"The results are out."

"What results, dear?"

The question disappointed me. I did not expect him not to know what results we could have been waiting for so eagerly and I was worried that something was wrong. He was drunk again. Did he have to go to the office drunk? Wouldn't that ruin his work? Why did he have to drink almost every day? I made up my mind to talk to him about it. I had seen what beer had done to my father and I wouldn't let it ruin my Jack. But no! Jack was far too responsible and caring to let liquor ruin his memory. That left only one explanation: He did not know who was calling. And this could then mean only one other thing: that there were other girls who called him. Jesus! This couldn't be! But it was.

"Are you still there, dear? What results?"

"Tell me frankly, Jack, do you know who is calling you?"

"How the hell can I, if you don't identify yourself? You all sound the same to me." I burst out in tears. I was so hurt I couldn't talk. Why should he do this to me? I wish it was someone else and not him. Why? Why? Whom did he think he was referring to as "dear" if it wasn't me? I looked up to see Miss Ironside, a white friend I worked with, standing in front of me, staring.

"Ironside, please, give me a break. It is hurting, it is. . ."

21

"I am sorry, Miriam. Anything I can do to help? Why don't you ask for permission to go home? The boss will grant you, please try."

"Please leave me alone. Do me a favour and go."

The good thing with Miss Ironside was that she was very understanding. She left reluctantly and went back to her office, just next to mine, all the time keeping an eye on me.

I didn't work that morning and I didn't call Jack again. The boss had granted me a day off, but I didn't feel like it; it would have been worse at home.

"I'll be alright, sir, I prefer here to home," I had told him. He said he understood and left. I didn't go for lunch, either; I just sat in my office, alone and lonely. I felt something was about to happen and no matter how much I tried to guess what it would be, I couldn't find an answer.

I was woken up by the ringing of the telephone. The time was 8.25 p.m. I had dozed off and had slept for about two hours. I answered, "East African Airways, can I help you?" My voice was hoarse.

"May I speak to Miriam Nyambiu, please?" It was a man, and there was only one man who could call me up at work. I sobered up.

"This is me, Jack. How are you?"

"Quite okay, dear. Have you heard about it?"

"About what?"

"What else have we been waiting for, you good fool?" he joked as usual. "The examination results are out. . .I want us to go and check."

You can guess how I felt, so guilty, that I started to cry again. How could I have judged this man, who was so concerned about me? I too had asked him the same question he had asked me, yet when he couldn't understand me I

22

condemned him. Feeling guilty I told him: "I am sorry, Jack, forgive me, please, I mean I shouldn't . . ."

"Now, what is all this? What am I supposed to forgive you for? You haven't done anything to be forgiven for. I have never known you to wrong me. Or.... or... you can't have failed dear. No! cannot believe that, not unless you want me to go mad".

I had to tell him the good news straight away. I could tell that he was now getting upset. "I got a First Division, Jack. The headmistress called me soon after she got the results." Man, the boy was relieved. I could tell on the line by the way he laughed.

"I am on my way to Embakasi, I'll hang around till you close for the day. Any objection?"

"Please hurry up, I'll be waiting."

When next Miss Ironside saw me, I was laughing loudly and hugging her.

I didn't look out for a car, because I did not know what make to expect this time, but I knew that he would come driving. And I did not wait long either. Fifteen minutes later I saw him step out of a Volvo. I hadn't taken lunch and I told him so, as I narrated the torture I had gone through after calling him. Our first stop was in a restaurant and after lunch he took me to a boutique, where he bought me a dress. In another shop he bought me a wristwatch and then a pair of shoes, all of which amounted to Shs. 2,200, the equivalent of two months' salary. These were presents for my good performance in the examinations and I accepted them. But it was something I could not encourage, for I did not want him to ever think that I loved him for his money, but for what he was: innocent and good looking, understanding, respectful, patient and loving.

Life as a working girl was good fun. Its beauty was

enhanced by having the best boy a girl could dream of. Mom had much confidence in me and she never bothered where I went after work. But I made sure that I never abused the honour and the respect she accorded me. I therefore never slept out. I didn't have many expenses and so we shared my income. When I realized that she took it reluctantly, I decided instead to be paying my sister's school fees, as well as paying for her other requirements. The maid too came under my payroll.

When the results came out, I was promoted and got a pay rise as well as being confirmed as a permanent employee. The E.A. Airways service vehicle then began picking me up for work every morning. My performance had really paid off.

Chapter 2

Jack and I got on very well. We had developed a habit of meeting everyday after work. The driver would drop me off at a pre-arranged place and Jack would pick me up. We would spend the better part of two hours together, then he would either take me home or ask one of his friends, who owned a fleet of taxis, to do it. On weekends, he would take me out of town to a place of my choice, or to a place that he felt I should visit.

The more I saw him, the more I felt the need to be close to him all the time. I had developed an appetite for his company and though I was with him often, I still felt there was something missing; I just couldn't get enough of him. I also suspected something else: that I was reaching a point where all that mattered to me was to be with him; learning from him; drinking in his knowledge of things that seemed unending. I wanted him for myself, to the exclusion of everyone else.

Wednesdays had become my significant days. It was a Wednesday that I first met Jack; on a Wednesday when I got a job with East African Airways and also on a Wednesday that I got a written promotion. On this particular Wednesday, mom let me know that she needed to talk to me, and from the look on her face, I knew that it must be a serious matter. It was my day off, and I waited for her to initiate the discussion, which she did at around midday. She called me to the room where she sold beer.

"Nyambiu," she called and then fell silent as if waiting for me to continue. I hated that moment, like all moments when my mom showed uneasiness. She continued:

25

"I have something to discuss with you and I do not know where to start from..." She stopped to look at me and seeing how I tensed to hear her talk that way, she added in a hurry: "I am sorry, dear, I don't intend to frighten you at all. It is not a bad thing. Do not think I do not know how good you are to me, but at times we have to talk. There is a young man who has been coming here for a drink and I have good reason to believe that you know him. I do not know whether he came to me before you had talked. If you had, it is alright with me. He was here last week, the day I met him with his friend in your room. He had come to request permission to marry you. I want to know from you whether you have knowledge of it."

Well, that was a hot one. It was hard to discuss this matter straight with my mom, but I was glad Jack had taken the initiative. It meant very much to me. I tried hard to face her but I couldn't and as she was waiting for my answer, I knew I had to say something. With my eyes focussed on the floor, I said: "Yes, Mother, I know about it."

"Thank you, that is what I wanted to know." Again she was silent for a few minutes, then she got up, went to the store and came out with two bottles of beer. She opened one and started drinking. I could see from her face that the idea of me leaving her was not a pleasant one, but she had known too well that sooner or later this would happen. There was nothing I could do about it. Even though it was still too early to make concrete plans, like naming dates, Jack and I longed for nothing more than the day we would finally begin living together as man and wife. Oh, to have Jack all to myself !

"Nyambiu," she called again. "Do you love this man? Are you sure he is the right man for you?" she asked, sadly. I could understand why she was sad.

26

"Yes I do, Mother."

"For how long have you known him?"

"Since I was in school." Surprise registered on her face. She certainly had not expected such an answer.

"Well . . .I must admit that I am surprised. I do not know what to make of it. I do not know what I can tell you, because you know too well that I did not expect you to have gone that far while you were still in school. You must then have been very lucky to have..."

I knew I had to talk now. I hated to hear her drawing wrong conclusions and unless I told her the truth, there was no way she would get the correct picture. I thought of what she meant when she said that "I must have been very lucky to have..." It could only mean that I was lucky to have completed school before becoming pregnant. That was not only bad, it was also an insult to Jack, who would never have tempted me into having sex with him. It hurt me to know that mom didn't know that I was still as clean as I was before Jack came to my life. I was emotional when I tried to explain.

"Please, Mother, there are some things I cannot enjoy talking with you. I'd hate to think that after all, you have failed to trust me. Mom, I do not know how I can put it to you . . . but try to understand that I am the same as I was when I wasn't going out. I am the same, Mom. Nothing has happened to change me."

I hoped she would understand what I meant. I didn't know how to tell her that I was still a virgin, or better still that Jack would never ask me for sex, and that he respected my purity. I wished she knew that the man whose integrity she was trying to question had actually guarded my virtue and without his protection I would have sunk long ago.

I knew I would have to choose my words carefully, as

27

I needed to be both courageous and respectful. She looked at me straight in the eyes for a few seconds and it was as if she was trying to detect evidence of my lying. Finding none, she addressed me: "Nyambiu, there is only one thing I would like to tell you. Your father was very nice to me before we got married. You'll probably find it difficult to believe. But take it from me, that he catered for my every need and wish. He was a sweet darling who never drank and would always be at home whenever he was not on duty. Now see what became of him and I. We are no longer together, no longer calling each other honey, sweetheart, handsome, beautiful, and all the other loving names. Those who knew of our love don't believe that we are now divorced. But, I also..."

"Please, Mom, please don't hurt my..."

"No, let me tell you," she interrupted me authoritatively. "You must know that I have more experience in life than you do, dear. I was telling you that I also know that all men are not the same. There are so many people who are happily married and if they had watched those whose marriages have failed they would never have married. I have no right whatsoever to make the choice of a husband for you, but I have every right, as a mother, to advise you, and no matter how badly I put my advice, you must not get hurt. You mean very much to me and until I am sure you are in the right hands after leaving me, I'll never rest. I was only shocked to learn that you have been friends with this boy since you were in school. But when you later told me you are the same as you were before you began going out, I understood. This tells me that your friend is serious about you. But let him prove his seriousness by arranging a wedding by which the world will know that you two are one. Nyambiu, do that as the last favour for me."

I promised her that I would. It was so small a favour to ask that I didn't feel Jack even needed to be persuaded about it.

I moved to Jack's home about four months after the discussion with mom. When I later thought of her advice, I saw clearly that she had meant well. She was trying to make sure that I wouldn't blame her if things between Jack and I didn't work out and if I was forced to go back to her with children.

We were now living together, not married, but with mom's blessings, until we were ready for a wedding. She had personally told Jack that she would never forgive us if we failed to have a formal wedding, and he had assured her that it would be the first thing we would do when we had saved enough. That was all the assurance she had needed, and I moved in with Jack.

Jack had a very nice and spacious place in Eastleigh. We packed my things in a suitcase he bought me. He proposed that I leave some of my clothes at home so that mom wouldn't feel I had left her altogether. I agreed with him and so I didn't pack everything.

My heart was racing like a horse as Jack opened the door to his house. He stood aside to let me enter the home which was to be mine from then till "death did us part". I felt different. I felt I now belonged to someone other than mom or dad. I felt owned, and completely belonging to Jack. I felt a different responsibility for this home from what I had in mom's home. I started imagining raising my children here in the company of Jack as their father. I was so overwhelmed I couldn't talk. I walked to the window, staring outside where the car was parked, our car. He walked over and touched me and I turned round to face him.

"Are you regretting being with me now? Aren't you happy any longer?"

"Don't be silly, Jack," I said as I fell into his arms. "I have never been so happy. Please take me somewhere to rest. Please hurry."

He lifted me up as if I were a two-month-old baby, carried me through to the bedroom and laid me on the bed. For the first time in my life, I was lying on a man's bed. And it was Jack and I, all by ourselves, locked in the privacy of this room. I felt his right hand reach for my breast. I thought that at that juncture my heart had given in; I thought that it had ceased its functions. The whole of my body became wet. I felt my breasts moving up and down as his soft hands went all over me. Then I felt something else; lips seeking mine. I was now breathing so heavily that anyone in the living room could surely hear. But there was no one to hear and I wouldn't have cared, had there been anyone. By the time our lips met, I was no longer in this world, I had gone out, slowly but surely.

I woke up at around nine o'clock the following morning. I had slept heavily, not because of the comfort of the bed, but because this was a new experience. I had never shared a bed with anyone, since I was eleven and the fact that this time I had shared it with a man was quite an experience. And, of course, that man was Jack.

Jack was fast asleep. I supported myself on one elbow and looked down at his sleeping face. he was breathing gently, his lips closed tight. I felt the temptation to kiss him and I found myself doing it. He opened his eyes and looked up at me, smiling. Suddenly, he grabbed me gently on the back of the neck and squeezed my lips against his. His hand started caressing me and I felt hot all over. I knew what would happen next, so I pushed him away from me, but very gently, and sat up. I looked at myself and wondered how on earth I had come to the state I was in — naked, with not even a brassier, and I couldn't remember undressing. Then memories of the previous night flooded back. The last thing I remembered was our lips coming together, then darkness. I must have fainted under his light weight. I looked at him and he stared back, smiling, as if nothing had happened.

"Did you have to do that Jack?" I asked him.

"Do what? I hope nothing wrong." Instead of a direct answer, I looked at my nude body then at him. He understood.

"Well, that was the best I could do. That's why you slept so heavily."

"Ooh, did I?"

"Yes, like a babe in its mother's arms."

"That makes you a hypocrite, doesn't it?"

"Well, it would depend on what you mean by *hypocrite.*"

"I didn't know we slept before three o'clock this morning. Maybe I was dreaming."

"Drowning in River Tana?"

"No, sleeping between the mattress and you."

"That wasn't a bad dream. I didn't hear any screams, anyway."

"I didn't say it was a bad one, Mr. Hypocrite."

"I don't think I like that name. It sounds bad."

"Neither do I, so kill it by stopping the pretence."

"I have stopped, but I hope you are alright."

"More than that, Jack, more than you can guess. I have been longing to have you all to myself, alone in a place like this and my dreams have come true." He kissed me and I jumped out of the bed.

I took a towel and wrapped myself in it. I went to the

31

living room and was surprised at what I found.

There was a bookshelf half-filled with books which I hadn't seen the previous night. Neither had I noticed the pictures on the wall and the colour of the sofa set, nor a coffee table set and a small chest of drawers next to the door through which I had entered. I was seeing all these for the first time, which went to show how much I had been preoccupied with him to have paid any attention to the surroundings.

I took a bath and went into the kitchen. In the sink there were six mugs, a good number of tea spoons, two kettles, and about six small *sufurias,* all dirty. He had used them and when they had all got dirty, he gave up cooking. It was clear that he never cooked anything else but tea. I pitied him, but then I remembered that was the reason I was here — I was to do his housekeeping. Odd as this may sound, I was happy that he needed me, that I could be of use to him.

On the way back to the bedroom a calendar on the wall attracted my attention. I went closer and looked at it, not for anything in particular but for the date. It was the 24th of August, a Thursday. This alone told me something: that the previous night had been a Wednesday. I looked around and saw my image in a mirror on the dresser. I didn't know what drove me to do it, but I looked closer, and the image in the mirror announced something to me. It was talking, telling me I was no longer a virgin. I didn't know whether to be happy or sad; to cry or laugh. But since I had lost my virginity to Jack, everything was all right.

"Where is my suitcase? Did you remember to bring it in from the car?" I had just remembered about it because I wanted to put on a fresh dress. I wished then I had looked for it before asking him. He jumped out of the bed, his face showing fear of some kind. He didn't even cover himself, but rushed straight to the window. I could see that the car wasn't broken into. He went back into the bedroom and put on some clothes. He then went to the sink and washed his face. After combing his hair, I saw him take a bunch of keys and go out. He brought the suitcase in and then addressed me:

"I must take this car back to the showroom. I'll be back in fifteen minutes' time." He took off, the wheels protesting against the high take-off speed.

On Thursday afternoon I picked up the telephone and called Jack's office. I felt there was something wrong, because he hadn't come home the previous night. It was the first time in the six months that we had lived together that he had spent a night out. I was greatly worried, as I had spent the whole morning trying to call him with no success. I got through to the office at around 3.30 p.m. Jack wasn't in and whoever was answering the phone was either very drunk or very sick in the head. He must have been mad. He wanted to give me a date, inviting me for a drink. He was telling me to name the place I would meet him within an hour, or at my convenience. I was so worried about Jack that instead of hanging up I put up with the foolishness, hoping that as we talked on he would be good and give me an idea as to where my man could be.

There was something that was puzzling me: every time I called this office I would hear the same music. This time it was even worse; there was so much noise that the man I was talking to was shouting, which also forced me to do the same, so that he could hear me. I was eager to know what had happened to Jack, and this made me restless. When I insisted on being told whether they were expec-

33

ting him back, whoever was talking told me that this was not Jack's office, and "....if he told you it was, then he lied to you. You sound young and ignorant and for this, I might volunteer an advice. Jack is a dangerous man and if I were you, I would forget about him. He has so many women that he wouldn't care whether you called or not. But I must caution you never to mention to him what I have told you. We both might live to regret it."

That speech really threw me into confusion. I hung up and a mist of thoughts clouded my mind. I could barely see what was in front of me. I tried typing and soon realized I wasn't succeeding. I realized too that I was about to break down and make a spectacle of myself in front of my colleagues. So I did the most sensible thing: I locked my drawers, picked up my handbag and called it a day. I took a taxi and was driven straight home.

The curtains were drawn and without doubt, I knew Jack was home. Although I was angry at his failure to call me, knowing how worried I would be, I was also excited that at least he was back home. I ran the short distance from the gate to our door. I wanted to see him, to make sure he was all right, to ascertain that he did not have any injuries on his face. The man I had spoken to on the phone had insulted him. He had insulted me too, by calling my husband dangerous. I had a feeling that whoever he was, he hated Jack and would probably have hurt him, beaten him up because, as far as I knew, Jack was one man who wouldn't fight a man or hurt any living thing, not even a louse, if it bit him.

The door to the living room was not locked, so I went straight in, ready to hold him and hug him and explain to him what had forced me to come home early and in a taxi. It was the first time for me to hire a taxi alone.

34

As I entered I was surprised to be met by five faces, four of which I didn't know. When they saw me, the faces of these four visitors were filled with fear. I saw one get up and grab a small bag which was on the coffee table and hold it between his legs. A second one snatched an object which was on the table and hid it behind him on the seat. They all turned their faces to stare at me; none of them talked. When they were satisfied that I was harmless they turned to look at their host.

"This is my wife," Jack said and turned to me, "I brought visitors home today. How come you are so early? Is there anything wrong?"

"Everything is quite okay, I'll explain later," I told him as I walked towards where they were seated.

Although these visitors were expensively and smartly suited, I felt ill at ease with their presence here in our home. They did not fit into any class of the people I knew. They had mannerisms of policemen, but when you observed them closely, they seemed a bit too expensive for ordinary police officers. Even in those expensive clothes they did not look like dignitaries. They didn't look like they had ever gone to school, yet they were not illiterate. They lacked personality but I could detect ruthlessness in their faces.

As I shook hands with them, I saw what the bag contained. It was filled with new currency notes. I did not betray my shock. I went into the bedroom to keep my handbag and it was when I was there that I overheard a conversation.

"What do you say, Master, should we continue?" one of them asked.

"Of course, she is alright. You can go ahead." That was the voice of my man, the one I claimed to know very well, but who I now discovered was known by others as "Master"

I hadn't expected Jack to have a nickname.

I did not know what to make out of all that. I peeped through the keyhole and saw them sharing the money between themselves. Something inside me told me that the money was not clean. There was no doubt about that.

In ten minutes I had made tea and served them. They had finished their work and the table was now cleared of the bundles of money. I looked at Jack and saw that he was uneasy, but he did not want to show it. From the way the boys were talking to him, I understood that they respected him. They were all happy and quite at home in our place now.

Whatever was happening I was only too aware that this was the first time we had ever received visitors here. I made up my mind to make the most of this rarity and I enjoyed entertaining them. I wanted them to stay till supper time, and I would make something special. Somehow I felt that they were Jack's protection, especially against the man who had talked to me on the phone. This thought alone made me warm towards them. They had faces which announced danger yet were not dangerous. They were people who looked like they could put up a fight, if someone provoked them.

I got up and Jack followed me into the bedroom. He held me from the back as I opened the wardrobe.

"What is all that hurry for! Are you going out?"

I think he said that to announce his presence in the room or just for the sake of saying something because I was in no hurry at all, nor had I shown signs of going out. I turned and faced him. The face that I saw this time was not the same face that I had seen when I first entered the house. This one was bright and happy; the face I was used to; the one I loved. The smile on this face told me that my

36

company was what he was missing.

"Is there something wrong with you, Milly?" he asked as he took my hand.

"Not at all that much. Do I look different from my usual self?"

"Yes, as if you are not pleased to see me. I am wondering why."

"There is nothing which pleases me more than having you around, Jack. I was worried when you failed to come last night. When I called your office, you were not there, and no one seemed to know where you were."

"What were you told when you called?"

"Oh, forget it, dear, it was bad news. The person I talked to was either very drunk or mad but most likely both."

The knowledge that I did not know my man well enough surfaced again. I had never seen him angry, so I did not know how he looked like in that state. During the time we had been together I never gave myself time to think along those lines. There hadn't been reason to. What I knew of him was that he was an innocent man, who cared not what the world looked like or thought of him; a self-sufficient person who had long known the secret of contentment.

Had I not been so blind in my love, I wouldn't have been taken by surprise. The telephone conversation earlier in the day with the man I had thought insane came back to my mind. He had said Jack was dangerous and now I suspected he must have been right. The moment I mentioned my disappointment, Jack's face contorted, exposing such danger that I could have sworn he had swallowed a live bee. A vein protruded on his temple, threatening to burst. Words failed his open mouth, and he stared at me with such fury that I said a silent prayer. What I was now seeing scared me so much that I knew if I were to talk,

37

he would do me harm. He looked like he could commit murder and think nothing of it. After several moments of searching for words, he finally put them together, insisting that I tell him what the man on the phone had said.

"Milly, tell me the exact words he used."

"Well, he told me you had many women and I shouldn't rely on you. That you are a dangerous man and..." I stopped, seeing that he was almost bursting with anger.

"And what else? Please go ahead and tell me."

"That if you had told me the number I called was for your office, you were lying." I gave him the whole story.

"Is that so!" he asked, more to himself than to me. I didn't answer. I only watched him as he left and joined his friends in the living room.

"You know what, gentlemen?" I heard him say. "That Kagondo man has lost one game. The first and last he will ever lose." Silence followed. Seconds later I heard their shocked voices, voices which clearly said that there was trouble ahead.

"What has he done?" one of the four asked.

"Imagine him trying to give my wife a date on the phone, when she called and also telling her that I had other women and I wouldn't care whether she called or not. He called me dangerous and told her that she should not take me seriously. If he doesn't spend three months in the hospital after I am through with him, then he'll no doubt live to see the end of the world. One thing I'll never do on this earth is to give anybody a warning. You wrong me once and I come after you. I'll never waste my time negotiating with an enemy, because in doing so I'll be encouraging him." He excused himself and went out of the room.

"That Kagondo must be mad. How dare he try a thing like that? He has picked on the wrong person this time,"

38

said one of the visitors.

"I think there could be a mistake somewhere. Maybe someone else took the phone. Kagondo is one man who could not play about with Master. He knows it would be suicidal. You don't go talking about Jack, unless you want to buy a new set of teeth."

They fell silent when they heard him coming. This surprised me as well. Here I was, worrying myself almost to death that my husband could be in trouble with that man I talked to on the telephone, yet the husband I believed harmless was now being talked of as a terror.

I pretended not to have heard anything as I collected the cups and took them back to the kitchen. I wanted to talk to the "terror" before he left. I was afraid he would get himself into trouble if he went out in that mood and I wanted to stop him, if possible. There was no doubt in me now about him being a terror. No one who talked the way he did could be classified as being peaceful. But terror or not, I was not afraid of him. He was still my good old loving husband.

"Mother of the young one," one of them addressed me, "have this envelope. Whatever is inside is for our supper. When next we come, we will spend a night here." I hesitated, but before I could get the right words to reject the offer, he had literally put the envelope in my hands. I took it reluctantly.

"Jack," I called as they reached the door, "I want to have a word with you before you go."

"I am sorry, Milly, it's getting late, not now please."

"Please, Jack, p-l-e-a-s-e." He looked at me and forced a smile, then came back.

I held him round the waist and pressed him against me. I made sure he came into contact with my breasts. I knew

39

he was annoyed because somebody had offended me and he was now going out to seek revenge. But I was also determined to change his mind. If only he would listen to me!

"Jack," I started, after kissing him lightly on the lips. "I was worried when you did not come home last night. I was worried when you failed to come in the morning; I was also worried when I called your office and no one seemed to know where you were. Please do not do anything to make me worried again."

"What is your worry this time, dear? I am with you."

"But you are going out for a fight. I am worried about what is going to happen between you and the telephone man. You might get hurt, dear. Please don't go."

"Milly," he called. His face now was somewhere between a grin and a smile, "I rarely get hurt. Do I have any scars on me? But I at times hurt those who offend me. I hate anyone who takes me for granted."

"But dear, you must learn to forgive and forget. The telephone man did not know who he was talking to. Maybe he meant to be good to me."

"What is wrong, then, in letting him know who he was talking to? You are the only valuable thing in my life, Milly, and anyone playing about with you might as well be committing suicide. You know."

"Please, Jack, please. Learn to forgive and forget."

"That is one mistake I'll never make."

"Which one? To go out fighting? I am glad, Jack". He smiled back at me.

"No! Not that one. To forgive, and worst of all, to forget. That is the worst thing I can do in my life. But for your sake, I promise not to hurt him. We won't fight."

"I cannot trust you, Jack and I am sorry to tell you this. You look like nothing in this world could stop you if you came face to face with that man."

"In that case, dear, I can't help it if you fail to trust me. How many times have I come to you limping?"

"How many times have I persuaded you not to go out?"

"Milly, when it comes to giving a question for an answer I am never amused. That won't get us anywhere."

"Jack..." I kissed him on the cheek before I continued, "do not leave me. I want you to stick around here until tomorrow. Please don't go."

The door opened and one of the visitors' face appeared. Seeing how we were engrossed in talk, he hid his face and called from behind the door.

"It is getting late, Master, and the Nyika is still here. What do you suggest?"

"I looked at Jack with pleading eyes. I tightened my hold on his waist and rested my head on his chest. Looking at his face I saw him smile and I knew then that he would not go.

"Okay, boys. Let's meet tomorrow, but take care that you don't cross bridges before you reach them. The market is hot right now."

He lifted me up and carried me over to the sofa.

"I hated doing things you don't like, Milly. I hate offending you. Please, I beg you not to be so strict in future. You might stop my heart from functioning and the result might not please you."

"I am sorry. I only felt you shouldn't go to town in that mood, you..."

"Forget about it dear. You have won, because you are nice to me."

"Thank you," I said and rested my head on his chest. His hands started their caressing work, and I knew that if I was receptive, we would sleep hungry. I jumped from

41

his arms and made for the kitchen to clean the dishes before I prepared supper.

"Milly," Jack called me from the living room. It was heading to 7.30 p.m. and supper was almost ready. I stopped what I was doing and went out to attend him. It was rare for him to call me while I was in the kitchen. I had now known why he never cooked anything, other than a cup of tea, when he was staying alone. Jack didn't know much about cooking. His style of making tea was laughable; he didn't like it hot and so all he did was to heat water, pour in the milk and when it suited his liking, he mixed it with tea leaves and drank it that way. It was tasteless, but he liked it. Another reason was that he never gave himself enough time to sit and eat. It was as if eating was time-wasting. But by now I had made him get used to sitting down for meals and he was enjoying it.

"Hello, dear. What's up?" I asked when I got to him. I was surprised to see that he had put on his coat and shoes, which he had earlier on taken off.

"Have you changed your mind, dear? Are you going out, after all?"

"Have you become a chatterbox, Milly? Who said I am going out?"

"A question for an answer. Have you forgotten what you just told me?" I reminded him.

"I am sorry, I do not have cigarettes. I want to go for some."

"I'll escort you, and then we'll come back and sit for supper; it is ready. Is that okay with you?"

"Not a bad idea, honey. I hope you'll say the same about sitting with me in a bar. I feel like taking a bottle of beer before anything else." He knew I wouldn't go in a bar and I knew this was a shake off.

42

"Why don't we take my small bag and fetch the beer? You can take it here."

"That would cost us a lot. If I sat alone here, I could easily drink two cases of beer without getting drunk."

"And in the bar?"

"Six bottles, at the most, and I would be through with it."

"And how many bottles do we have in one case, if I may ask?"

"Twenty five, fifty in two cases."

I burst out laughing. The difference was unthinkable and yet he looked serious!

"You know, Milly, we men prefer places filled with cacophony; discordant places if you know what I mean. The clattering of glasses as they fall from the tables and from the hands of drunkards; people screaming out at each other and at times fists flying and bottles thrown; calling the waiters by whistling and at times insulting and pushing them about as if we've married them. I assure you in a bar when one is on his sixth bottle he is drowning. See what I mean? Now make your choice."

From what you have just told me, dear, and I take you seriously, I'd rather have you drowned by the two cases in my presence than have you risk your head colliding with a flying bottle."

"But you seem to forget one very important thing, dear."

"And what is that?"

"Ninety-nine per cent of me has spent his life in such places, that is, long before we met." I knew when I was beaten.

"How long will six bottles take you?"

"Give each bottle ten minutes and an extra allowance of thirty minutes at the end."

"That makes it one and a half hours. I grant you two,

at the most."

"Thank you. That's a deal. I'll avoid places where there are women, I hate them."

"That is your funeral. Now, can you please go, you are boring me."

"I was just about to tell you the same thing. What a bore!" He went out.

He knocked on the door as the 9.00 p.m. news had just started. I let him in, took his hand and led him to a seat. Not that he was staggering, but I had to show concern. I switched off the radio, but I remembered clearly that just before I did, I had caught a news headline: *Five armed gangsters raided a Nakuru bank today morning...* Such news never interested me, but for some reason, this particular piece registered in my mind...

We took our tea-break at 10.30 a.m. Most of our staff took the opportunity to look at the newspapers then. I joined my friends at a corner when they were reading the *Daily Nation.* I wondered what was so interesting in the news, because almost everyone was busy reading. I saw that they were reading about the same robbery that had been broadcast over the radio the previous night. Not to look out of place I joined in the meaningless fun. Some surprised me when they expressed admiration for the robbers. ".... These people tried. With that kind of money (Ksh. 215,000) the five can start a business and give up theft..." For something to do while we slowly took our tea, I too read the item. I got interested as I continued, but my insterest was different from that of the others: something was telling me I knew more about this than what I was reading. I studied the descriptions given by the eye-witnesses and slowly the pic-

44

ture came into focus: it fitted the five people I had served tea at home the previous night. Although it was almost incredible, I became more and more certain that this was a reality rather than a coincidence.

I took my tea in a hurry after the realization that my suspicion could be proven right. I felt certain that my friends' eyes were on my back, though when I turned to look at them I found them engaged in their own things. Still, I felt as if they knew what I really knew, as if they could sense I had seen the money being shared out and had got a share as well. I excused myself and left.

Back at my desk, my mind now focussed on what I had witnessed the previous night. Things I seemed to have ignored or dismissed in the past now started to come back to me in sharp perspective. It became clear to me now that I must have known what Jack was all along, but ignored it because I didn't want anything to destroy our relationship. The unquestioning acceptance that Jack worked at DT Dobie, for example, and the telephone number that could have been anywhere else but in an office, didn't surprise me now. I only felt hurt that he saw my innocent faith in him and deliberately led me on.

My mind went back to the day we had first met. I remembered the innocence on his face; his soft manner of speaking; the self confidence; patience, and best of all, his doubtless good advice. I found it hard to believe that he wasn't real. But hadn't the questions lingered in my subconscious all along? If it was true that Jack didn't work for DT Dobie, then where did those different cars he drove come from? He said they were company cars; which company? Then this telephone number I had been calling...there was always music in the background, at times quite close: sometimes there is so much noise that I have to shout. And why did Jack always sound drunk when I talked to him on the phone? He even slipped once and told me that his office was a crazy place, when I mentioned the music.

Could he be working in a bar? Of all things I am sure Jack could not be a barman or waiter, cashier, or whatever other ranks there were in bars. So the only explanation there had to be was that he had given me the telephone number of the bar he frequented. But....Jesus this could not be true. If he doesn't have an office and probably isn't employed, what else could he be? He has money alright and yet he doesn't have the qualities of a businessman: And if he was a businessman, why had he never let me know? Businessmen like to talk about their work, so why hadn't Jack told me about his? Or maybe he didn't trust me?

My thoughts took me back to the day I first entered his house and we had left the suitcase with my clothes in the car. When I reminded him of the suitcase, he had jumped out of bed and rushed to the window. At that time I had thought that he was worried that the suitcase might have been stolen, or the company car had been broken into. But later, it occurred to me that he had almost panicked. He had dashed out and sped off in the car and had come back within minutes. I remembered wondering how he had managed to reach town, hand over the car and come home within such a short time; it was as if he had driven only two streets away.

Back in the office, I took the newspaper again and read it carefully. The description given of the gangsters fitted the visitors I had served on the day of the bank robbery. I was now sure that they were the robbers. I had caught them sharing the money and they were frightened. I had walked in on something that was certainly not meant for my eyes.

I read on: *armed with pistols and simis*. Well, that object that had been hidden must have been one of the guns. There was no doubt about the whole thing now. If Jack wasn't working with DT Dobie, then he was a robber.

I put the newspaper aside and took the telephone directory. I wanted to make sure that I was not accusing him falsely. I looked for DT Dobie and found it. There was no number corresponding with the one he had given me. I then remembered the name he had mentioned to his friends when he said that the man had missed a game. He had called him the 'Kagondo man'. I looked up 'Kagondo' in the directory and was surprised to find the name Kagondo Bar, and the number was the same as the one he had given me!

The realization that the man I loved so much had lied to me shocked me. I loved him not for his money or the cars he drove, or even where he worked, but for himself. His simple self. I had felt right deep inside that he would mean a lot in my life. But I certainly was not thinking about sharing his criminal life. There was no doubt that what the Kagondo man had said was true. The only mistake he had made was to try to date me. I now understood why he had cautioned me against telling Jack what he had told me. Yet I had, ignorantly, put him in trouble. I pitied him, but there was nothing I could do about it now. After all, I concluded, he shouldn't have had such a loose tongue.

The knowledge of my husband's occupation had suddenly changed my life.

I stood up as if I had suddenly realized that I was sitting on acid. I found myself locking the drawers, taking my handbag and walking out of the office, without informing anyone. I came back to my senses when I came face to face with the boss.

"Excuse me, sir. I was coming to your office. I have just received a message that I am required at home immediately. I . . . I . . . do not know what . . ."

"It is okay, Miriam, you can go and see what it is. Just call, if you need any help." The boss was white and very understanding. But I had lied to him, I was stammering because that was my first time to tell a lie. I felt guilty and annoyed with Jack. Had he told me the truth from the beginning this, I was sure, would not have happened and I would still have loved him.

I took a taxi and went straight home. I needed time to think and this called for privacy. Jack had made a liar of me, he had made me a party to his loathsome deeds. Yes, I was in trouble. I could not leave him and go back to mom. I still loved him. My love for him told me that he would need my help, or just my presence, badly and so the thought of leaving him was out of the question.

I thought I would attempt to persuade him to try and stop being what he already was: a violent robber. But before I talked things over with him, I decided I would play dumb for a while. I wanted to make sure whether I was still in love with him or not and whether I would go on loving him even if he changed for the worse. For who knew what lay ahead for me? He could change and become wild, spending nights out; he could also become violent, or other such evil. Could I go on living with him if he was all these on top of being a robber?

He was home when I arrived. He opened the curtains when the taxi stopped outside our home and I thought I saw him smile at me. He met me at the door. His welcome this day was somewhat unusual. He came to me with open arms and encircled me. He kissed me on the cheek, released me and took the jacket I was carrying. I, of course, forgot

48

all my prior thoughts and the only thing that mattered right then was to be in his arms. He carried me to the sofa, but I was already on him, giving him the hottest kiss he had ever known. We held each other, kissing deeply as if our lives depended on it.

"You know what makes you so nice?" he asked me when we got a break.

"I don't, tell me please, Jack."

"You come into my life just when I need you badly. You are always punctual in my life, always turning up on schedule."

"And what else? Tell me something else. Anything else to make me feel I am all yours."

"Yes, there is another very important thing which I think I have told you before. I mean...there is no need of repeating, is there?'

"Tell me again, even a hundred times. I'll want to hear it..."

"You came into my life when I needed you badly. God meant you to be a gift... His gift to me, a gift I'll never let go, and believe me, Milly, nothing will take you away from me, I won't allow it."

"I am overjoyed to hear that, Jack. You have never spoken such sweet words before. I don't know what I can say about it."

I had started stammering. In fact whenever I was face to face with this man I never got words to express my real feelings. The things I had decided to tell him vanished. All I could see now was the man I had known when I was in school: the innocent Jack Zollo, who couldn't hurt even a fly. Right at that moment I didn't care what he was. Robber or no robber: a salesman or not; he was mine and the only one I would live to an old age with.

49

Chapter 3

Life had now settled to a normal routine. I had got used to Jack's frequent late nights, even the occasional nights out. He had not done anything to remind me of that awful day of the robbery and consequent newspaper reports. He still came home often in the so-called company cars. Sometimes he would park them outside our gate, but often he would leave them down the street. Visitors were still alien to our house, and the four he had been with on the day of the robbery were the only ones that had ever set foot there, at least in my presence.

On this Saturday morning, I woke up to do the morning chores while Jack had his beauty sleep, the result of another late night. Later in the day we were to go and visit my mother as well as deliver some books I had bought for my brother and sister. It was almost 10.30 in the morning and Jack was still asleep. I'll never know what moved me to go over to the chest of drawers where I had kept the books at that particular time.

I took the books out and a matchbox that must have been somehow covered by them caught my eye. Jack never used matches, only lighters, for his smoking. I wondered what it could have been doing there and I reached for it. But it was too heavy for an ordinary matchbox and my curiosity got the better of me. I opened it and what I saw were certainly no ordinary matches. How could they have been so heavy? A closer look told me that the matches were too few in number, resting on a thin cardboard fitting nicely into the matchbox. I poured out the matches and removed the cardboard.

Packed to fit snugly in the bottom of the matchbox were six capsule-like objects. The tops of these objects were rounded off, like real capsules, but the bottoms were nicely cut to a flat base, as if the capsule had been halved. But what capsules! They were a dull gold colour and were it not for their weight, which led me to the conclusion that they must have been made of lead, I would have thought that they were little gold nuggets, unpolished of course. Studying one closely, I noticed some numbers inscribed on the flat bottom. Now, of course, my imagination ran away with me. What other wonders was my husband hiding in our house?

Like the naughty child who will hunt for more treasures once a little is sampled, I ventured back to the chest of drawers and this time I was making a conscious search. I pulled open a drawer and encountered a paper box similar to the kind that pieces of chalk are usually packed in. It was marked "chalk" and I wondered what in the world Jack would have wanted with a box of chalk, unless he had taken to tutoring classes when I was away from home. But on lifting the box, I knew that it contained no such thing. It was just too heavy for ordinary chalk, however many pieces it may have carried.

This time the capsules were slightly larger than those in the matchbox, but matching in shape and colour. I was so absorbed in studying them that I did not hear the bedroom door opening. When I looked up, Jack was standing there. He could not have fully taken in what I was doing, for he was smiling tenderly at me. The smile, however, vanished as soon as he cast his eyes on my lap and saw his chalk box open, and a few samples of the heavy capsule-like objects in my hands.

"Put that down at once, Milly. Who told you to open

the box? What were you looking for?"

"Oh, Jack, are there things in this house that I should not know about? I thought we understood..."

"Oh, Milly. At least listen to me this once, my dear. Do you know what those things are?"

"Maybe a new type of chalk. They were in the chalk-box," I said, trying to sound light-hearted about it, for I could see that he was greatly troubled.

"For God's sake, Milly, stop being such a mug and put them back." He was now on his way to helping me pack them. "These things are dangerous, poisonous. You should never have touched them in the first place, and certainly not with your bare hands. Put them down, wash your hands and come back with a handkerchief if you don't have gloves."

Why don't we use yours, dear? Please go for them while I rush to wash my hands," I told him in faked urgency. I knew it was hard for him to imagine that I would have the slightest idea of what they were.

"Now look, who told you I have got gloves?"

"Well. Considering the risks involved, I cannot imagine you without a pair."

"So what do we do? I do not have any."

"So? You stop hiding things from me. When will you know how much you mean to me? If you knew these things were dangerous why didn't you warn me so that I keep off them? Now, be a good boy and tell me what they are."

"They are called pistons. They belong to a friend who wanted them for his car. But he won't need them any longer, anyway."

"Why not? You put it as if he is dead." I only said this to earn time. I knew he was lying.

"He sold the car and bought a new one."

"Jack, please. For how long are we going to live this way?
You know it hurts me to hear you lie. You are not a con-
vincing liar, Jack. You hate it and this is why you aren't
fooling me. I do not see why you should force yourself to
lie to me."

"What is the lie this time?"

"These are not pistons or whatever else you may think
of calling them. If my guess is right they are bullets. These
big ones are scribbled 9mm. At least you should know that
I read novels and James Hadley Chase knows more about
these than you do." He smiled shyly. I knew I had cornered him.

"What would I need bullets for, Milly? I am not in the
army."

"Let's not talk about that. The fact is I know they are
bullets. Now tell me, do I need gloves to put them back?"

"Well, I am sorry that you have to doubt me. Anyway
leave them to me."

"So now I don't need to hurry and wash my hands?" I
teased.

"That depends on the hygiene you were taught in school,
if you ever got the chance."

"I never went to school, Jack. I guess that was why you
thought I was so stupid as not to know what they are."

He packed them back and after taking a bath, he joined me for breakfast.

"Do you remember that we promised mom we would
visit her today?"

"Yes I do. I'll be at Terrace Hotel from 3.30 p.m. You
can come for me when you are ready to go."

"Can you manage a company car? 3.30 will be late."
I asked knowing that he now knew he couldn't fool me any
more about anything.

"A company car on Sunday? Don't be silly."

"It won't be the first Sunday you have borrowed one. Last . . ." I sensed danger and skipped the subject.

I arrived at Terrace Hotel at around 3.00 p.m. At the stairs I met two men coming down and from the way they were walking, it was easy to tell that they were very drunk. I was afraid that they would make a pass at me. I hated going into bars. Jack knew it, but once in a while he would force me to meet him at a bar. In such cases he always made sure that he chose a place he regarded as being safe and quiet. The two men tried to block my way and I stopped in my tracks. Seeing that I was afraid they got encouraged and came directly at me. One got hold of my hand by force and shook it violently, while the other one provided the greetings. "Hellow babe, why are you so wild? Come on. You came here to fetch money. What kind of man have you in mind?" He looked at the other and told him: "This one is good for me, Sam, what do you say?"

"Go with her. A hundred bob for this one is not a loss."

I pushed him away and he went staggering down the stairs. When he got up from where he had fallen, he came at me screaming blue murder. I had never been so afraid. I tried to scream but no sound would come out.

"Scream as much as you like. Who do you think will come to help you? Give her time to scream, Charlie."

I didn't have to be told the men were toughs; it showed all over their faces. I was so scared that I wished a miracle would happen. Where was Jack and why wasn't he coming to rescue me? Then I heard footsteps approach from behind and blessed God, praying that whoever was coming would be a good Samaritan. A man and a girl appeared. Sam was still holding me and Charlie had just slapped me on the face and was calling out insults. I was crying. The man stopped by and asked:

"What is the matter, young men? Why don't you talk to her politely? She'll understand."

"*Mzee*, go your way. Is she your daughter? Are you going to refund me the money I have spent on her while she has refused to keep her part of the bargain?"

That alone sent me raving mad. It was an allegation that I knew would stick, especially in a place like this, where I was not known and Jack's presence was not certain. I freed my right hand and hit him in the face with all my might, sending him crawling down the stairs on all fours. The man and the girl, sensing trouble, took the stairs two at a time and I was left alone with my assailants. Before Charlie got up from where he had fallen, I pushed his drunk colleague away and before they could recover, I was taking the stairs up two at a time, just like the man and his girl.

I could hear their footsteps as they came running after me, shouting insults and warning me they would get me no matter where I went. I reached the restaurant and caught sight of Jack, seated with a friend, drinking. I made straight for him with my assailants following close behind.

Jack's friend saw me first. He must have immediately realized that there was trouble, from the way the men were coming after me. He stood up quickly, causing one glass to fall from the table so as to alert Jack of possible trouble, then walked over and stood between me and the two men.

"What do you think you are doing, Charles? Do you know who this lady is?" he addressed one of the men.

"Captain, I do not care who or what she is, or even whose she is. The fact is, she must pay for what she had done. Whether I die in the process or not."

He pushed Captain aside to try and reach me, but before

55

he could get closer, Captain grabbed him again. Other drinkers had now noticed the fracas and were attentive. Some had even left their seats and had come closer and I could see they liked it. A man came from the furthest corner and addressed himself to Captain.

"You people make these prostitutes have big heads. Let Charlie get his woman and go with her."

"Any woman coming to a bar without her husband is a whore. Who can claim her? She is for me, you, and anyone else who feels like it," another quipped. I couldn't stand it any longer. I laid my head on the table and started crying.

Jack was quiet all through, I saw him light a cigarette and look at the two men who had talked. His eyes were red with anger, and I was afraid he would get involved in a fight with these toughies who were now ganging up. I put my right hand on his thigh and begged him: "Please, Jack, let's get out of here, I do not want . . ." He wasn't looking at me. He was staring at Charlie, puffing his cigarette and causing a cloud of smoke. He spoke to Charlie.

"Charles, what did I hear you say? Can you repeat whatever you said?" He then turned to the gathering people.

"And anyone who doesn't want to get involved with this coming murder should get as far away as possible." He turned back to Charlie, "I am still waiting for your answer."

A good number of those who had come closer moved away. I sensed that those who remained were Jack's friends, who were ready to assist him in whatever was to follow. Charlie was still in Captain's grip. I was surprised to see how he had abandoned his pride and cooled down as he talked to Jack. I looked at his face and saw it was a bit

56

swollen where I had hit him. Part of his right eye was bloodshot.

"Jack," he called with respect, it is this lady; see what she did to my face? And she has spent a lot of my money. When we reached the stairs she refused to go further." I couldn't say anything. I didn't believe I was hearing right but he was telling it without fluttering an eyelid.

"Just a minute, Charlie," Jack interrupted. "You want to tell me you've been with this woman drinking together . . . I mean . . . do you want to tell me you have bought her beer?" He was speaking with that soft voice of his which feigned peace and innocence. I was to know later that he was at his angriest when he talked that way, not when he looked deadly.

"Yes . . . from 10.00 a.m this morning. We started at Rwathia, with her and Sam."

"Is that so, Sam?" he asked my second assailant.

"Yes, it is true. We were seated in the inner bar. Don't you remember seeing us, when you passed to go to the toilets?" I watched and listened silently. I pitied these two for what would happen when Jack's anger unleashed. But even more, I pitied the women who spent their time in bars, if these were the type of men they dealt with. Jack then turned to Captain and said: "Do you hear that, Cap?"

Captain didn't answer, instead he asked Charlie: "Do you know this lady?"

"Why should I? She invited herself to our table and I had to..." He did not get further. I saw Jack's right hand move and Charlie was on the floor. It happened so fast that I did not see what he hit the man with. Charlie then tried to sit up from where the blow had sent him and as he did so, Jack hit him all over the body with the heel of his shoe, so hard that he had no chance of getting up. Jack

57

looked murderous and I was afraid of trying to stop him. As he went again for Charlie on the floor where he now lay, he was held from behind by a waiter who had come from the counter.

"Please, Master, do not start this thing here again. Can't you figure the loss it will cause?"

"Did you hear the story he gave me? And do you know who this woman is? He says he has been drinking with her since ten this morning. By that time we hadn't even got out of bed. How dare he do that to my wife?"

"I am sorry but I didn't know it was that serious. Why can't you call the police? He can be charged with assault."

Jack didn't take any heed, instead he went to where Charlie lay on the floor and kicked him again, making him roll over.

The waiter pleaded again: "Please don't con . . ."

"Come any nearer and you'll wish you never met me in your life."

The waiter went away. Jack then turned to Sam, who on sensing danger headed for the stairs. In a second he was in Captain's hands, having it really rough. No one intervened. All seemed now to have changed their mind and were on my side. I heard someone say: "Do you want to tell us we will never bring our wives in bars because of you? Our wives must be shown where we go and you young people have sat on our shoulders so that we cannot risk bringing them here. Okay, have it from your equals."

What worried me was that when Charlie sat up, he was holding two of his teeth in his hand. I had heard stories of people losing their teeth in a fight, but I did not know that it was so bad. I felt pity grip me. Despite the embarrassment the two had caused me, they didn't deserve losing their teeth. I got hold of my handbag and stood up.

A man who had earlier on said I should be left to Charlie beckoned me. He didn't seem wild at all now, as a matter of fact he looked afraid.

"Is Jack your husband or only a friend? Please excuse me for asking."

"He is my husband. Why?"

"Because if that is so, then things won't stop here. You are now the only one who can stop it. Have you ever seen him fight?"

"Never, I am even surprised he has done it. I couldn't..."

"Then, mother of the young one, if you do not want more and worse surprises, take his hand and lead him out of here. Please..."

I went and got hold of Jack's hand. I knew what the man meant and I was sure he was right. As his wife, I was the only person who wasn't afraid of him right then.

"That is enough Jack, let us go. Please stop it there."

He didn't argue. He left the man and we headed for the stairs. The waiter caught up with us at the top of the stairs.

"Captain," he called, "who was paying for the bill?"

I realized I was involved with dangerous men when, instead of answering, Captain hit the waiter on the nose and sent him to the floor bleeding. And as if nothing had happened, Jack took my hand and led me out.

"If it wasn't for your presence, we would have gone on until the police were summoned," he told me as we reached the street.

No mention of the fight in the bar was ever made after that and although the memory of how devastating Jack could be was ever present in my mind, there had been no reason to discuss it. But on this Sunday morning, the scene replayed over and over in my mind as I digested the news that Jack had just given me. After having met Captain the previous day, Jack came back home to announce to me that he would be going out of town to visit a friend.

It had been a couple of months since the first encounter with his friends and traces of the money from that robbery were beginning to disappear. Jack was a big spender, living lavishly and showering me with gifts all the time. I had known for sometime now that he would run out of money, and was wondering what he would do next to replenish his dwindling resources.

His announcement of a visit out of town did bring the robbery, his denials and the fight in the bar back to mind. Although I did not voice what I was thinking, I made sure that I checked whether he had taken the match and chalk boxes with him. The matchbox was gone and the chalkbox was half empty. When saying goodbye that morning Jack was in such a hurry that he wouldn't even sit down for breakfast. His mood was foul and not even the forced smile could hide it. I dared not broach the subject of my suspicions.

I could not work that morning in the office. Images of what Jack could possibly be doing haunted me constantly. The robbery which I knew was taking place at that particular moment became so real that I worked myself into a real illness. I asked for a sick leave at lunchtime and went to see the doctor, who gave me two days off.

Back at home, I was faced with the emptiness of the house and the fear that my husband could have been injured, arrested and in police custody or maybe even shot dead. Along with my fears for him, were also worries about what could happen to whoever would stand in his way, for would Jack stop at anything to achieve what he wanted? Woe be unto the teller who would refuse to hand over the

60

money, or any security guard who would dare lock the door in his face. Scenes of gunshots, wounded bodies bleeding all over a bank floor and total confusion were flashing before my eyes, as if I was in a movie theatre. Yet, in it all I could not see who had won the battle, the good guys or the bad ones — in this case, my husband's gang. It was too much, and realizing that the silence in the house had something to do with my imagination running away with me, I switched on the radio, partly for background noise, partly to catch the news of the possible robbery, when VOK announced it in the hourly news bulletins. But I heard nothing. I couldn't bring myself to go to bed, so I tried to concentrate on a novel that I had picked up from the chest of drawers-cum-armoury. But instead of following the story, what I saw was Jack being chased by armed policemen. He dived into a river and was having difficulty in swimming. He was shouting for help from onlookers on the banks but all they did was to laugh at him. Police bloodhounds were swimming fast behind him and as the first one dug its fangs into his head, I screamed.

I woke up to find that it had all been a dream. The time was 3.30 a.m and I decided to go to bed.

I got out of bed after a restless sleep at about 9 a.m. I switched on the radio but again news was not forthcoming. I decided to go to the kiosk for milk. I hadn't reached the kiosk when the headline of the *Standard* newspaper on the pavement where the paperman sold his wares caught my eyes. Hurriedly, I threw money at him and did not wait for change. I grabbed the paper and tried to read and walk at the same time, towards home. I must have been quite a spectacle, because I remember a man asking me if I needed help for, as he said, I looked sick. I declined his help and realized that I had to get home before I started screaming right there in the street.

I straightened myself up and walked straight back home where I threw my *kiondo* down, sat on the sofa and read the whole story. "FIVE-MAN GANG ROB MACHAKOS BANK: 2 dead, 3 escape in police shoot-out," the headline screamed at me. The gangsters had been stopped at a roadblock and had refused to stop, at which point the police opened fire. They had given chase and the gangster's car had been shot at; it rolled twice and landed in a ditch. Two men had been shot dead, while three had escaped into the nearby bushes. But the area had been cordoned off, the paper said, "and there was no hope of the three robbers getting away with the crime". The robbers had got away with about Shs 175,000 from a KCB bank in Machakos. Their description again fitted the only visitors whom I had once entertained with tea.

I was screaming and crying out loudly. Jack was in trouble. My fears and nightmares had come true. What was to happen to him? And me? "Oh Lord, please, please save my husband!" I was overcome with despair and sadness and was beside myself with worry. I must have gone on my knees for I remember praying loudly: "Lord, in the name of Jesus, your only son, who came to this world to save sinners, please save my husband. He is a sinful man, a robber and a devil. Lord, please take away the evils in this house. Clean Jack and give him the desire to live an honest straight-forward life. Lord conquer the devil in my Jack..."

I don't know how long I beseeched the Lord to save my husband, but when I looked up from my prayers, I knew that the devil was really in our house right then. I could not believe my eyes, for sitting there opposite me was Jack, calmly blowing smoke rings into the air. How long he had been sitting there, I could not tell. But one thing I knew:

that he had heard my prayers, and from the look on his face, he must have considered them as useless as a bottle of whisky in a bishop's party.

We stared at each other for a long while and I saw that he wasn't going to break the silence. The onus fell upon me.

"Jack, tell me, my dear, how did you swim out of that river before the police dogs caught you?"

I was confused. I couldn't tell what I had read in the newspaper from what I had dreamt. But Jack just stared at me and wouldn't speak. I was getting frustrated. How could he not tell that I had been going through hell, thinking of him and his safety? Was he just going to sit there blowing smoke rings in the air and staring at me?

"Jack, please tell me. How did you get away?

When he decided to respond to me, it was not in answer to my question.

"Milly, tell me, have you mistaken our house for a church? Would you tell me the devil you were referring to in those prayers? Has someone been harrassing you while I have been away?"

"No, Jack, no one has disturbed me."

"Then what was all that talk about? And what trouble was I supposed to have swum away from?"

What could I say? Jack was evading the issue and torturing me in the process. We both knew what I had been talking about, but he wasn't going to admit it.

"You know, Milly, it takes a soft heart like yours no time at all to go mad and I don't want that to happen to you. Let's try and understand each other. Are you sick? Would you like to see a doctor? The way you are staring at me tells me something is awfully wrong with you. It's as if you have been hypnotised."

Now who was fooling who? Here was the Jack I had seen

63

being shot with guns and mauled by dogs as he was swimming in a dirty river and drowning. Yet he was sitting right there in front of me? Could I really be innocent of the robbery that even the paper had written about?

Jack, my Jack. Away for 36 hours, a whole day and a half, during which I had tormented myself with all sorts of imagination as·to the nature of danger he must have been facing. My Jack, who must have been out of town, visiting friends and all along thinking of his Milly and her safety. And now he was here, as concerned as ever about my safety.

I got up automatically, as if a switch had propelled me to where he was sitting. I threw my hands around him and ignored the bulge in his inside pocket that pressed against our bodies. I held him to me, eager to protect him from all the evils I had imagined might have befallen him. I never wanted to let him go. I was weeping silently, this time not from fear, but with joy in the knowledge that he was safe and with me. I squeezed him so tight that he gasped for breath. I eased my embrace a little.

"Jack, I had a bad dream. I dreamt that some bad people were chasing you across a river and you didn't know how to swim. You screamed for help, but no one would come to your rescue. You were drowning and..."

"That's a nice dream, dear. I like its spirit. You know, when people don't like you, you shouldn't like them either. And that gives you the courage to hit back effectively when the time comes."

I could not believe my ears! The man was joking about nightmares and giving no thought at all about the hell I had been going through on his account. But wait a minute, that was the typical Jack that I had come to know — the one who never allowed little incidents like dreams to run the day for him. My Jack, my worry-proof Jack. The only thing that would really worry him was the person or thing that would dare come between him and his Milly.

"Jack, you don't have to sleep out without telling me. It is not very bad but it worries me."

"That is good news, dear, I am amused."

"What do you mean? I am very serious, Jack."

"I know, but it is great to know I have someone somewhere who worries and cares about me. But tell me, who was the devil you wanted your Lord to chase away from here? The way you put it shows that you had a particular person in mind."

"I was praying... I had to. I felt..."

"Do you normally pray in the living room, with the door wide open? Who were you praying for?"

"For...for...you. I could sense you were in some kind of trouble."

"What kind of trouble and why did you think I would be in trouble?"

Without knowing it, I looked at the newspaper on the coffee table. I saw him follow the direction of my eyes and his face paled. He picked it up and became so engrossed in it that he forgot I was there. I watched him from the corner of my eyes as he read one paragraph after another. He took out a pen, sat down and did some calculations. He divided 175,000 by six, after subtracting 10,000. He then added two shares together and I saw his face light up with what I thought was satisfaction. His must have been a double share probably because he owned the gun, but I couldn't be so sure. When he pushed the paper away with a smile he remembered I was around and it almost surprised this rock of a man. As if the newspaper and what he had read had nothing to do with what we were talking about earlier on, he asked me: "You haven't answered my question, Milly, what was the trouble and why did you think I would be in it?"

It was hard to know when I had caught Jack off-balance. A few minutes ago, he had reacted to my gesture when I had looked at the newspaper. He had known what I meant and it had been proved by the calculations he had done. Yet now we were back to square one: hard questions. I remained quiet. I did not want to volunteer more of my suspicions lest he came up with more and harder questions.

"Milly, dear, if you go on worrying yourself, thinking that I am in trouble, because I failed to come home, you'll worry yourself to the grave. Would you like me to risk getting attacked by rogues and wild animals by coming on foot when my car develops a mechanical problem? Would it please you to see scratches and cuts from wild animals and rogues on my face?"

"I am sorry, Jack, but I...I thought I saw you carry some of those things you called pistons." He smiled. He understood I was up to something and he was giving me wider ground to manoeuvre.

"So what if I carried them? Is that enough reason to worry you? What do you think I carried them for?"

"I thought they would protect you in case of an attack. People fear them."

"Why? How can I use them?" I knew we were fooling each other and I liked it because in the process I knew I would hit the point.

"You simply put them in your gun and fire. I know the theory of the whole process."

"You are becoming interesting, Milly. Who told you I had a gun and what do you think I would need one for?"

"What is this hard object protruding from your coat?"

66

That ended the whole game; I had caught him red-handed and he knew it. He had forgotten that he had it on him and that I had felt it as I caressed him between talks. He stood up and headed for the bedroom. "You can go to hell, Milly," he said jokingly as he closed the door behind him. Three minutes later I followed him to the bedroom. From what I saw, I needed no more evidence to prove my suspicions of his involvement in the robbery.

On the bed was a big heap of money, in new currency notes, which had not passed through many hands, if at all it had ever left the bank. He was sorting the money out, heaping the notes separately: hundreds, fifties, twenties, and the few tens there were. I knew he was counting what he had got away with. Words failed me. All I could do was stare, as if I had not seen money in my life before. It was as if it would talk to me and tell me it had been stolen from Machakos.

Of course, I had seen money all my life, but never in such large sums and all for one person. I found myself wishing that the money would be put to good use — that it would be given to someone who would invest it for profit. But even as I entertained the thought, I knew my wishes would come to nought: those who knew how to invest money wisely rarely ever got it. Luck went to the desperate, the careless and the extravagant.

I looked at the money, the beautiful invention of man, which had turned the whole world crazy; money, that had motivated my good performance in school and hence the good job that I held. But it was the same money that turned people into murderers, robbers, prostitutes, conmen and conwomen. It made many women become shop-lifters and petty thieves; it created jealousy and lust. Money made man hungrier than his Creator intended him to be. All this

67

became clear to me as I beheld the display of currency on our bed. I moved my eyes away from its beauty.

Chapter 4

I was going home from church when I met Captain. He was walking between four men and I could judge from the look on his face that he did not enjoy the company. There were two others behind them, I could not tell whether they were together, but it was easy to conclude that somehow they were all in the same group. To me they appeared to be more of police officers than Captain's regular associates.

I slowed down as we neared each other, I was sure Captain could not pass without saying hello to me. I stretched my hand to greet him and at first he pretended not to know who I was. All of them stopped. The two who were a few paces behind, reached us and stopped. When they realized Captain was not willing to shake hands with me, one of them talked.

"Why don't you greet your friend? Don't you want us to know her?"

Captain's answer surprised me, but by the time I realized what he meant, it was too late. "She's not my friend, I do not know her, I have never even seen her and I guess she is mistaking me for somebody else."

"Do you know this man, young lady?" one of them asked me. I wished I had given a negative answer. But in order to prove myself smart I admitted knowing him.

"When did you know him?"

"They came with my husband home."

"Who is your husband, I mean what is his name?"

I saw Captain look at me and wink. It at once struck me that these were police officers and he did not want me to mention the name of my husband, Captain was right

then under arrest and had probably been forced to direct
them to where Jack stayed and did not want to do so. But
as Captain winked, one of the officers noticed. That alone
brought trouble. I was confused. My first thought was to
give them a name, a phoney name and so I said: "He is
called Bonnie Mwangi."

"What does he do? I mean where does he work?"

"In town, with DT Dobie."

"Do you know that we can arrest you for telling a lie?"

"I am not lying to you, why should I?"

"Do you mean if we go to town right now we will find
him on duty?"

"Just call the company and confirm, they'll tell you
whether he is in or not." Although I had some fear in me,
I wasn't going to allow them to scare me stiff. I knew I
was not guilty, and knowing Captain and whatever he did
for a living didn't mean I was guilty of an offence. I waited
for the next question. I was decided not to tell them any
truth. I had sworn to protect Jack and I was going to do
it at whatever cost, even if it meant telling lies.

"Where do you stay with your husband, young lady?"

"Call me Mrs. Bonnie or Mwangi but not young lady,"
I said boldly.

"Okay Mrs. Bonnie, where do you stay?"

"On Eleventh Street, plot number 4243, door number
6." That was one place I had never been to and I hadn't
the slightest idea whether there did exist a plot with that
number. I knew they too didn't know and was almost certain that they were not going to ask me to take them there.
One of them took out a notebook and a pen and made
me repeat the number, which I did. I was afraid that I
would contradict myself, as the number had just entered
my mind at random. Well, whether I did or not, they too

had not noticed.

"Mrs. Bonnie," the one who seemed to me more senior than the rest called. "I have no doubt that you are a nice woman, all I would tell you is to try and avoid associating with characters like this one. Do you know what he does?"

"Well, if he is nice to me I do not see why I shouldn't talk to him."

"Wasn't it about two minutes ago that he pretended not to know you? Can you guess why?"

"That's what I mean, Mr...Mr..."

"Sang." He helped me.

"Yes, Mr Sang, what I was saying was, when he pretended not to know me I forgot about him." It was a good lie.

"This man is a robber, do not let him get involved with your husband much. Anyway, I'll try to visit the number you have given us, this evening or tomorrow morning."

"That was that, I knew what his visit meant and I was glad I had thought of giving them a phoney number. I crossed the street and headed in the direction away from our home. I was feeling uneasy, for I knew their presence in this area meant trouble for Jack. I had left him at home doing nothing and I was afraid he would get bored and decide to move a bit. It would be risky, because the places he visited most while at home were around the very area the police were already combing. I wanted to reach home quickly and warn him, but this long route I was following would make a great difference. I had no doubt that my hurrying attracted attention: I was half running and half walking. I happened to look back to see how far away the cops were so that I could turn and head in the right direction. I saw that two of the cops were following me, at a distance. They wanted me to lead them to my husband, which made me realize that they had not swallowed my lies.

71

My heart started its racing which I thought sounded like the hooves of a horse running. I didn't know what to do. For, not being very familiar with this area where I resided, I knew of no short cuts which I could use to dodge them and then run to warn Jack that hell had broken loose.

A matatu that had just stopped to drop commuters gave me an idea. I thanked the angel who had made me take the direction I had followed. This matatu went round First Avenue to Second Avenue, where our home was. I looked behind and saw that the cops were out of sight. I had gone around a corner, entered a lane between two blocks and emerged on the other side, where I now saw the matatu. I jumped in and it took off.

I kept looking behind, although I was sure the cops had not seen me enter the matatu. I remember hating matatus for speeding but right now I could only compare this one with a tortoise. It was funny that the woman I sat next to was claiming that the driver was overspeeding. In less that five minutes, I was at Wood Street. I alighted and ran the fifty metres home.

Jack was a funny man. While I was worrying myself to death and running in the streets, he was comfortably sitting on the sofa, his legs stretched on the coffee table. A Thermos flask I had filled with tea as I went out, was beside him on the floor. He was completely relaxed.

"Hey, Babe," he called loudly as I entered, "you look cute, it seems you've been having a nice time somewhere. I have drained your Thermos." He started laughing and funny enough, the laughter was not a forced one. He seemed to be in a very quiet, relaxed mood. I looked at him, just as a mother looks at an innocent baby and without intending it, I put my arms akimbo, to look at this ignorant "Son of Fate". He looked straight in my eyes and winked;

72

sometimes he was like a baby. He also seemed to feel protected in my hands, and my presence always seemed to give
him inspiration of some kind. Before I said anything, I
found myself laughing too. What for, only heaven could
tell. In most cases when there were only the two of us, we
tended to behave and even felt like school children.

"Jack, ever been told that you are a good fool? Has
anybody ever been kind enough to tell you that? It would
be a favour."

"I doubt whether they have been born."

"Who?"

"Those who can have the courage to tell me that. Anyone
telling me that had better talk to a grave-digger." Again
he started laughing; it was as if what he said was a
laughable matter.

"Then here I am. I have let you know, but I am sorry
I haven't talked to a grave-digger, so please spare me."

"And that is what makes you different from the
others...Ha! Ha! Ha!" I went and sat beside him, a mist
of thoughts crossing my mind. Just a few metres from where
we were was trouble, trouble enough to part me from him
for days, weeks, months or even years. Here was this husband of mine, looking relaxed, without the slightest worry
in the world; feeling protected by something he couldn't
even tell. Telling him of what was happening outside the
door would change his mood, would set him worrying and
uneasy; a thing I wouldn't have liked to happen, for I liked him the way he was right now. But he seemed to have
read my thoughts, and realized that I wasn't with him in
the house, though I did not show it.

"There is something worrying you, dear; tell me."

"But I am not worried, not in your presence. I am only

73

a little tired."

"In that case I'll go for a walk, while you rest a bit. I am also tired of sitting here all morning."

That started me off. I knew he would go and that was the last thing I wanted him to do. I told him: "You know...but promise me one thing before I tell you."

"What is it?"

"That you won't leave here the whole day."

"That will depend on what you'll tell me. It is a decision the two of us should make when we both know about it." He was no longer in his good mood. He was a man who sensed trouble before he got into it. I decided to tell him. After all, he was right when he said we should both know before we decided. I shouldn't have made the decision alone.

"Captain is under arrest. I met him near the church..." I gave him the whole story up to the time I entered the house to find him relaxed on the sofa. He listened carefully, not interrupting, till I had finished and the worry on his face was gone. He then sighed with relief and stood up.

"Milly, dear, Captain is the best friend I have and I can't let this happen to him. I must go."

"Please, Jack..., please don't. I'll die of worry if you leave this place, knowing what it is like where you are going."

"Do me one favour, Milly."

"What is it? But please do not ask me to let you go out."

"Remember what I told you some months back? I hate offending you and when you insist on some things which I know too well how to handle, you'll soon lose me. You'll put me into so much trouble that you'll wish you had never interfered. It might be too late then to regret."

"I am sorry, Jack. What was the favour you wanted?"

"Give me one thousand shillings. Will you?"

"Yes, but please take care." I stood up and went to my locker. There was just about enough money, which meant that I would be left with three hundred shillings. All the same that didn't matter, what was of uttermost importance was Jack's safety.

When I went back to the living room, I caught him red handed, wearing his gun. He tried to hide it, but I let him know that I had seen it. If anything, I was not going to allow him to carry that one. It meant that he was heading straight into trouble with the police. I couldn't stand that.

"Here is what you asked for." He took the money and smiled shyly at the thought that I had seen the gun. He knew I would talk about it.

"Thank you, I'll be back in ten minutes' time."

"But why the gun? Why carry it if all you are going to do is to buy off Captain's release. You won't go with it."

"Now, Milly..., I am sorry, anyway. I did not want you to see it. Should we go all over that again?"

"All over what?" I asked. I wasn't happy and I wasn't going to pretend to be, just to please him.

"Let me tell you one thing you've never taken time to consider. And this at times makes me wonder why you people read the Bible. It clearly tells you that under the sun there is everything and everything has its purpose."

"The Bible reader..." I thought. And he couldn't get the words to express his meaning which I had already guessed.

He continued: "There are two things in this world which go together. And the only two things that work out things perfectly are peace and war. When there is no war there is peace; when there is no peace there is war. By one of these two things I'll get Captain out of trouble. This money you've just given me stands for peace. This rod I have carried stands for war. I can assure you that with either of the two, Captain will be free within minutes. Have these two things, Milly, and you'll inherit heaven as surely as the meek."

There was nothing to argue about that. When Jack believed in something it was useless, and probably suicidal, to try to make him believe otherwise. He walked out of the room after I had wished him good luck, which I was sure he needed very much right then. But he didn't look or seem worried; it was as if he was going out to buy some cigarettes. I took the Thermos flask, the cup Jack had used and the rest of the dishes he had brought from the small cupboard and after cleaning them up, I got back to the living room. I knew that with Jack in what I assumed was trouble, I wasn't going to have any rest.

I sat down and as usual when I had something bothering me in mind, I started imagining queer things. The trouble was that I never saw Jack out of trouble. I always imagined him in the deep of it, and this always reminded me to pray for him. I could not fail to think that Jack was stupid enough to try to shoot at the police in trying to save the life of his friend, Captain, a man who was described by the police as a dangerous robber. What would stop the cops from shooting him, if he went anywhere near them? What if they caught him with the unlicensed gun? Wouldn't that be an offence in itself? Then probably the gun would be proved to have been used in various robberies. Wouldn't they charge him with more offences?

I do not know how long I sat there thinking and asking myself questions to which there were answers. When I looked up, it was to answer a knock at the door. When I opened, Captain was standing there, smiling. I did not know what to make of it. I stood aside to let him get in.

"Where is he? What happened? Is he in trouble? Tell me, Captain...the real truth, please. I can't go..."

He didn't have to answer. Jack emerged and touched me from behind. I jumped. The first thing that I thought was that the police had tailed Captain, without his knowledge and now I was being arrested. Jack turned me round and kissed me on the mouth. I opened mine wide to accept whatever goodies he was delivering to me. I got hold of his waist, ignoring the presence of Captain and before I became conscious of whatever we were doing, we were on the floor. I didn't know who had downed who. All I knew was that Jack was now on top of me.

"I told you, Milly," he told me as we sat down, "there was nothing to it. Here is Captain. How long did I take?"

"You took years. I hate you."

"Thank you for being so frank. Here, get back your money."

I didn't know what to think about Jack. It seemed he knew his way about this world of crime. I was sure he had taken more than thirty minutes. I looked at Captain, for whose life my husband had taken a risk and started remembering the time I had met him in the company of the police. He was then helpless, unhappy, miserable and worried. He had looked so ugly that you would think you were looking at an old shoe. He now looked relaxed, happy and without a care in the world.

"Mama," Captain called me, "you are a great woman. You saved my life. I hope you understood why I pretended not to know you?"

"I understood, but I am sorry it was too late. You know..."

"You did a wonderful thing, especially when you went the wrong way. I thought you would come straight home and I was sure that they would follow you."

"How did you get out of it?" I was eager to know how he had been freed, because I had earlier on been told that there were only two ways to do it. And I was sure one of them had not been used, since the money I had given for a "peaceful release" was given back to me. Before Captain could talk I heard Jack say: "That, Milly, is not your business. The less you know about it the safer you are. You had better give him something to swallow rather than ask questions. I am sure he is dying with hunger. That place is no man's home." I left them and went to the kitchen.

Captain left for town after supper, which was around 7.30 p.m. When Jack came back, he went straight to bed. The good mood he had been in that morning had been swallowed by either Captain or his rescue. That night he did not want stories; he wanted to rest and think and I let him be.

I sat in the office doing nothing but thinking. It now seemed as if I lived in the world of thoughts. When I was not worrying about Jack's safety I was worrying about myself. There was no doubt that his love had driven me crazy. I could guess why: if it wasn't for the fact that I had not known any other man before him, it was that I was intended to be his. There were times when I thought that had I met other men, probably I would have known the difference. But right now, I had no one to compare him to since he was the one person who saw me through school life, and the same one who saw me through my teenage.

It was about nine months now since I moved into his house. Things had started taking a new shape. We had promised mom that we would prepare for a wedding when we had saved enough money. She had started insisting that we keep our promise, but looking at Jack I could tell that there was nothing like that in his mind. Things were bad on my side for I realized that I was pregnant.

This had come at a very odd time. Jack had of recent become restless. He stayed indoors most of the time and I knew that he did not have money; a thing he hated to be short of. I also learnt that he was at the top of the "wanted list" of the police and adding my troubles to what he already had was a thing I could not bring myself to do. I wanted him to be calm, to feel free and protected. So the best I could do was to keep on giving him money; all that I had saved from what he had given me and from my own salary. It was enough to keep him indoors for six good months, with drinks. But Jack was not that type. The most he would ask for was twenty shillings for cigarettes. I would leave five hundred on the bedside locker for him as I went to work and when I returned, he would have used only fifteen shillings or none at all.

I considered all these facts as I sat on my desk and decided not to tell Jack that sleeping on me almost daily had brought about an as yet invisible third party to our home. So, for the first time, I visited a clinic and the third party, perhaps a would-have-been future king, was got rid of. But I felt I wasn't guilty; I convinced myself that it was yet another strategic move I had taken to protect my Jack. Though I had sworn not to tell him, I couldn't stick to it. When he was in a good mood one night, I told him the whole story. I was helpless before his eyes.

The whole of that week I kept on feeling helpless, uneasy and worried, as if I was expecting something bad to happen to both of us. It was an odd feeling, because in most cases I worried when Jack was out, especially if I happened to hear that some outlaws were in the hands of the law.

This time Jack was always at home, going out to the shop for cigarettes only in the evenings and coming back straight away.

My worries worsened when he told me one evening: "Milly, I have a very bad feeling. Something bad is going to happen to me. I have kept indoors all this time, trying to figure out why the police are so hot on my trail and no matter how much I try, I just can't figure it out. I have become impatient, I can't take this any longer. Tomorrow I must go and find out from friends. I am telling you, because I do not want you to start worrying yourself to the grave. But I must go. I cannot live this way and I do not want any objections, because, Milly, when a person like you interferes and I fail to take heed, I go straight into trouble.

"You shouldn't have told me then, because you knew that I must object.

"Okay...dig your own grave, because I must."

He was really worried; he looked like somebody who had swallowed a live bee and was being stung inside. I knew what would cure him right then. I got hold of him and kissed him. I caressed him the way he did to me, touching every sensitive part of his body. By the time I was through, he was in dreamland. He woke up two hours later, happy and looking relaxed.

We went out of the house together the following morning. When our service car came, I boarded it and he went across the road to take a bus to town. I wanted to withdraw some money from my bank as it was a Friday and I had promised a friend that we would go to her place outside the city the following day.

At around eleven thirty, I asked the boss to grant me permission, which he did. I arrived in town at twelve. I was about to cross Kenyatta Avenue when I saw a car coming at a very high speed and just then, I heard sirens from different police 999 squad cars. The traffic lights were red but at the speed the runaway car was going there was no possibility of it braking on time. Another car coming at right angles had now got the green light to go ahead. Everyone who was around the area opened their mouths wide to witness the accident which all believed was going to take place.

As the second car reached the intersection, the runaway car was dangerously close; its headlights were on, hooting like mad, making us almost deaf. When it reached where I was, I saw the driver. It was none other than my husband, Jack, being chased by four police cars.

I remember screaming so loudly that everyone turned their attention to me. I saw the picture of Jack behind the wheel: a wild look on his face, his hair standing upright because of the wind that entered through the open window. I waited, holding my breath, to see him crash into the other car, which had skidded to a violent halt.

By the time Jack's car reached the spot, my eyes were closed. I plugged my ears with my fingers so as not to hear the loud bang which would leave me without a husband. But even with ears plugged I could hear the police squad cars sirens as they passed by.

I do not know for how long I remained thus. Then I unplugged my ears. I was not yet ready to see the corpse of my husband. I heard someone remark: "Lo! He has made it! Whoever he is, he can drive."

That alone brought me to the world again. I opened my eyes. Jack had made it, so far, but the cops were still on his trail. Even without being told, I knew the matter was now even worse.

I saw a group gathered at the place from which the speeding cars had emerged. I was sure they were talking about it and that they probably knew what it was all about. I headed straight there. The only eyewitness had already given the story and left; the others were giving second-hand information and the more it was narrated the more the story lacked sense. But there had at least to be a gist of truth in it. All I gathered was that Jack had been spotted by police officers, who asked him to stop. They weren't armed, so he refused to stop and took off on foot.

Just then, the police stopped a passing patrol car and Jack, realizing he was going to get cornered, took out a gun and hijacked a whiteman's car. He forced him to step out, then grabbed the keys and took off just as the police car reached him. Knowing that he was wanted by the police (why else had he stayed indoors for weeks?), I was inclined to believe the story.

Having seen the chase with my own eyes, I couldn't believe Jack was safe. There were many police cars involved and the thought that he would outsmart them all seemed incredible. That, I believed, did not depend only on expert driving; it needed unlimited good luck. I doubted whether he had all that!

From that place I went straight home. The events of that day had upset all my plans. Even those of my friend had gone down the drain. I knew I couldn't do anything until I had known the fate of my husband. I wouldn't see the outside of our home until Jack came back.

When I boarded a bus, I was surprised to hear some people talking of the chase. Those who were along Ronald Ngala Street said that the car had knocked down a pedestrian and that to avoid the jam along the street the driver kept right, his headlights full on to warn other drivers of an emergency.

The curtains of our house showed that Jack was already home. I couldn't believe it. How could he have managed it? With fear and joy in my heart, I opened the door, which was not locked. He was there, lying on the sofa as usual. It was hard to understand Jack. When you thought you knew all about him, he did something else which told you that you knew but very little.

He stood up, smiling broadly, and came to meet me. His face announced happiness and satisfaction of some kind. He held me and pulled me to his chest and I felt the hands caressing me, from my head down to my hips, going far down to my thighs. I remembered the tender touch of his hands as I knew them during my school days. I remembered the day he broke through me, the first day I went to bed with him and how I had passed away to the invisible clouds under his light weight; how he had removed me from class 'A', the class of virgins, to class 'B' of the married. The thought that he had turned out to be a confirmed criminal, who seemed to enjoy every minute of danger, disgusted me. But there was this thing in him: all the qualities of a good and responsible husband.

I felt my body becoming weaker and weaker as he continued to caress me. In another minute the same invisible cloud that always hid us from the world of reality came to us. My knees gave in and I found myself on the floor. He came down with me, and by the time the cloud had vanished, it was heading to four o'clock.

I made tea and sat with him at the table. "Tell me, Jack, how did you manage it?"

"Manage what, for God's sake? Have you been dreaming again about the dogs, the unco-operative people, and the wide river where I was supposed to be drowning?"

83

If I hadn't witnessed the incident with my own eyes, I would have believed I had dreamt the whole thing. He had asked the question in a way which showed complete innocence. It was as if he hadn't even left the house any time of the day.

"Jack, please do not reveal a new chapter about yourself to me. Let me stick to the little that I know about you."

"And what do you mean by that, dear? *You* know little about me? Who on earth then does?"

"No one, not even me, and it might take ages for anyone to know you. I mean, even when someone is quite sure of what she is talking about, you are able to change her mind. For instance, Jack, I...I... was in town when what I am talking about happened. I saw you in that car. I was a few metres from the traffic lights on Kenyatta Avenue. Now when I ask you about it, you act as if you have been sitting here the whole day and almost making me believe I am wrong."

He smiled and held me. His lie didn't mean anything to him even with the knowledge that it had been proved to be so.

"I am sorry, dear. I didn't want to go to prison and leave you alone. I had to save my life. Someone pointed me out to the police. Did you read about that Nakuru bank-raid last month? Another beast swears that I was the getaway driver." I looked at him, looking sad as he tried to prove his innocence about the particular robbery. I pitied him, not for his innocence, but for the troubles he took to try and convince me that he wasn't there.

"Well," I said, "the man could be right. And if he is, there is no need of..."

"You are another one, Milly," he said as he stood up and started to look for a newspaper. On finding it, he came back to the seat. On the front page was the headline:

84

GANGSTERS RAID NAKURU BANK. He told me:
"Have a look here, dear. What date did it take place?
Remember where we were the previous day? The date here
is 15th and the paper talks of 'Yesterday' which was 14th.
Now go to the calendar and check where we were, if you
can't remember."

It surprised me how criminals could prove their alibi.
I remembered we had gone to a wedding party, where we
had spent the night. But that didn't mean that he wasn't
a robber; it only explained that he didn't participate in
that particular one. I pushed him a bit further. I liked the
way he was trying to prove his innocence and I enjoyed
to see him show signs of regret for his criminal life. I said:
"Oh, sure darling, that proves your innocence..." I saw
him relax. I added: "What of the Machakos bank? Where
were we? I was on duty, and you?"

He smiled, bringing that topic to an end. "Dear, it is
useless to prove one case while you are guilty of another
of the same kind, same style, same sentence if you are
caught up with, and same..."

"You can tell that to the monkeys, Milly. If you have
so much concern why don't you get me a job with the East
African Airways?"

"As a what? Bring any certificate you have...oh yes, give
me your driving licence, they need a driver. I'll..."

"Me! To become a driver? Going around every estate in
Nairobi collecting people and taking them to Embakasi?
And some of you, dressed like angels, stay in Mathare, but
when you are in the offices and crossing the streets wearing those miniskirts with stinking perfumes, one might think
you stay in heaven. Go get yourselves a good driver from
the slums. He'll have respect for you people. He'll go to
his knees to make you happy. The best I can do to such

85

women is give them a nice screw and..."

"My God! Jack, you can't talk that way. I just can't believe those words are coming from your mouth."

"I am sorry, I didn't put you anywhere there, did I?"

"Of course not, dear, but isn't that language dirty? I can't imagine..."

"Don't tell me I have formed a new language. It might make me feel great, you know?"

That was that. It was his way of bringing an unpleasant thing to an end. And when he did it, everything got back to normal again.

Chapter 5

I had gone to bank some money Jack had given me a few months back when a robbery had taken place. It was at the Bank of Baroda. Jack's luck, as far as I was concerned, seemed to be running out. I had started seeing very much of him in the wrong places; in places I was sure he wouldn't have liked me to see him. This was one moment I hated in all my life.

I had arrived at this bank at around 9.45 a.m. I took a form and sat down at the furthest corner and started filling it out. At around 10.00 a.m I heard a gunshot. Without more warning I went to the floor. I put my handbag under my belly and lay on it. I did not want to know what was going on, but I knew it was something horrible, though I had not expected it. Two men next to me also joined me on the floor. I heard one say in Kikuyu: *"Ngoma ici igutura ituthumburaga. No no ruriri ruitu."* (These devils will harass us forever. And they are our people).

Another shot echoed loud, making all of us almost deaf, then a voice: "This is a hold-up. All of you lie down, your foreheads against the floor." I was in that position already and I wondered whether there were others who were up to that time still standing. The voice continued: "Do not try any funny games. Just keep cool." Although the voice was different from the way I knew it, I could tell I had heard it more than a million times. The difference must have been caused by the harshness it tried to feign. Then another voice, which I also knew called: "Lenny, jump over the sixth counter." The voice belonged to a man once introduced to me as Captain.

When one of us at last stood up from the floor where we were having a forced siesta, the bank raiders were five minutes gone. I did not see any of them, and I wondered whether there was anyone who had. The confusion which had erupted after the first gunshot had turned us blind.

I didn't bank the five thousand I had; there was no time for that. The police came immediately.

I looked at the faces of the bankers, the faces of those who had been forced to lie down flat on the floor, tasting the dust and breathing with difficulty. I looked at the faces of the police which announced danger and dislike for the action, and then looked at my face, which appeared faint on the glass wall. It was as pale and as full of hatred as all those I had seen in the bank on that day. I felt something different get hold of me; some kind of hatred. Well, I had long proved that my husband was a robber, but I never cared; I still loved him, despite the fact. However, there was no time at all that I had approved of what he did. I never liked imagining him as a criminal. This time I felt strongly against the act. I wouldn't stand for it, even if it meant the end between me and him. It was bad to experience the same loathsome treatment he gave others; innocent people just like me.

I felt guilty of an offence; an offence some of whose fruits were right then in my handbag. The money he had given me had no doubt been earned by this same method. I felt like throwing the money away. But something told me that the best thing I ought to do was to give him the money back, thereby telling him I'd never want a cent from him if it were earned through unfair means.

I got out of the bank. I was stopped by a police officer who told me: "Excuse me, madam, could you please hang around for a minute?" It was a very polite request, but right

88

then I felt mad with Jack. I wanted to meet him and fight him physically or word to word. I said: "I am sorry, sir, I didn't see a damn thing. It was horrible. The whole..."

"Take it easy, madam. What we want is someone to help us try and get hold of those beasts. An eye-witness. Just give us some description of any of the...."

"Please, sir, just understand... I mean, how can you see the face of a person when you are lying down with your forehead to the floor and all the threats that if any of your muscles move 'you'll stop a bullet'? Telling you that I saw any face would be lying and I wouldn't like to do that." I had become hysterical. I felt like swallowing Jack, the whole of him, and keeping him in my stomach, because I felt Jack was not safe to be free. The inspector let me go. I didn't feel guilty for not telling him that I did not only see the faces, but that I very well knew at least two of the raiders. I didn't hate Jack so much as to give him away to the police. My duty was, instead, to protect him, though right then I felt like strangling him.

He wasn't at home when I arrived. I opened the door and got to the place where I always did my thinking, the same place where I had said prayers for this lost sheep. I sat down. This was the place where I knew happiness; the place where the worldly life was revealed to me, and the same place where all my sorrows got me.

Unlike other times, I now saw Jack moving about in the streets, his pockets bulging with stolen money. I saw him coming home safely, smiling as if he hadn't done anything wrong. I started talking to him. "Jack, I am telling you this once and for all: If you do not stop that game, we are through. I cannot stand this any longer. It is shameful, it makes me feel guilty and I have had enough of that guilty conscience. I was going to bank this money you had given

89

me. Then you beasts came in and harassed innocent people. Why can't you find something respectable to do? Even
the wives of shoeshine boys feel proud of their husbands.
Every husband is important to his wife, no matter what
he does for a living. Come on, Jack, you must change for
the better." I argued with him, without hearing a word
from him. I saw him nodding his head every time I told
him anything. Then I went out....

I woke up very late in the evening, my heart beating
rapidly and loudly. Jack had not come. I went to the
bedroom to see whether there were any signs of his having
come and gone. There were none. I went back to the seat,
this time worried that after all I might have been wrong
in thinking he was safe. It then occurred to me that every
other time I thought of him, I always imagined him in trouble. This time I had thought differently. Could it be the
opposite?

I went to bed at 1.00 a.m. after he had failed to turn
up. I did not go to work the following morning. In the
afternoon, Captain came. Seeing he was alone, I almost
got a heart attack. I could sense that he had brought me
bad news, though he had never done it before. No one had
ever brought me bad news about Jack ever since I had
known him. I ushered him in.

"Jack is under arrest. He is in..." That was all I heard
then. I could hear him talking, but not what he was saying. I screamed, tearing up the rasta threads on my head.
Tears were flowing incessantly. I was jumping up and
down, going to the floor the same way I had done when
they robbed the bank. I started hating myself for cursing
him, for saying he was not safe to be free. I was the cause;
I had something to do with his arrest.

Captain gave me time to cry myself dry. When there were

90

no more tears, he came to me and touched me on the shoulder. "Please, Mama, you had better listen. Crying won't help, not even if you commit suicide."

I listened. "Tell me quickly, what shall I do? Please tell me," I begged.

"He is at Central Police Station. I want you to go and see him."

"Will I be allowed to see him?"

"Of course, they won't give you any trouble. The police are good people. They are bad to those who are bad. Not to people like you."

"When did this happen?"

"Last night. I am afraid if I go to see him myself I'll be arrested. I want him to tell you what he wants. The trouble is, he cannot tell you everything because the police will be present when you talk with him."

"My God! Why do you have to do these evil things, Captain? Don't you people realize the problems you put your wives into? Now what shall I do if he is sent to prison?"

"Look, I want you to take what I am about to tell you lightly. It might hurt but unless you give yourself some extra courage, it might not work."

"Just tell me. I am sorry for..."

"Okay, just take it easy. I have tried the best I could. In most cases, we are able to buy our way out of such places. But your husband's case happens to be very, very sensitive. He is involved with a man called G.B. A man who has been on the wanted list for years. I am afraid the two of them are the best harvest the police have ever had in years and no man can be allowed to go near them unless he is proven to be innocent. Tell me, Mama can you take a risk for Jack? I mean would you do anything to save his life."

"Please tell me what you want me to do and I'll do it.

Forget about the risks involved. Without him I am finish-ed. I love that man, Captain, I adore..."

"Okay, Mama, go and buy two loaves of bread and bring them here."

"But Jack doesn't eat bread. He takes..."

"I know him better. Please just do as I ask you."

When I had brought the bread, Captain took both and opened the wrappers very carefully. He then took a letter from his pocket and put it on the table. "You can read it if you want. But if you ask me, I wouldn't allow you to do so," he told me as he took one of the loaves and started working on it. He opened its bottom carefully by cutting it at the centre with a razor blade. He took out some amount of the soft insides and through the hole he squeezed in the letter. He did the same with the second one and in-serted another letter. He then asked me for some wheat floor which I brought and which he mixed with some warm water. He applied the solution to the place he had cut and each of the bread was sealed again. You couldn't notice the cut unless you were informed and looking for it. He carefully wrapped both the loaves again. On the paper he used a different gum. They looked exactly the same as when I had brought them from the shop.

"Buy some soda on the way. Take this to him and his friend. Leave the rest to them."

Chapter 6

I made tea for Captain and as he took it, I went to take a shower. I did my hair, selected my best dress and put it on. I wanted to look smart. Jack had once told me something which stuck in my mind: "Milly, if you ever want your things to go without much ado just make yourself look presentable; dress expensively and smartly and even if you do not have money on you, you'll be surprised at how people give you way. You'll be accepted in any society. You will also be surprised how the title 'Madam' will be accorded to you. We have a very ignorant society, dear." From my past experiences I had proved Jack's reasoning to be very true. One good thing is that he had made sure he had bought me the type of dresses he had in mind, dresses I could not afford with the money the East African Airways gave me.

"Phew!" whistled Captain, when I came in from the bedroom, "...you'll make them sweat, Mama. They won't attend to anyone else before they are through with you."

"Who? What do you mean?"

"I mean... when you look so smart, whoever you are visiting in the cells will be accorded some respect by the police officers on duty. On the other hand, you do not look suspicious, and whatever you are carrying right now might go through without being closely inspected. See what I mean?"

"Thank you," I said for the sake of it. I hated anyone commenting on the way I was dressed. As far as I was concerned, it was only my husband who was supposed to admire me.

I approached Central Police Station at around 4.00 p.m. From what Captain had told me, I knew I was taking a risk. He had put it clearly, that in most cases, even the food brought packed, straight from the factory, was forced open at the station and the bearer made to taste each item.

"If they unwrap the bread and happen to notice our trick, you'll be in for a charge and a very serious one at that. Though they might not listen after the discovery, I would advise you to say that you had no knowledge of whatever was in the bread. Just tell them that it was I who gave you the loaves. Do not mind using my name. I am also wanted and that simple incident won't change anything. Only, do not be forced to say you can have me available."

Well, that is how good criminals are to one another. Captain was ready to have his name disclosed to put me clear of trouble, but he was frank enough to tell me that it was only a lame excuse, I would only use it as mitigation in court, because that was where I would end up if the trick was discovered.

My heart was skipping beats every minute as I approached the desk. There were four police officers at the desk. The oldest of the four had three red stripes on the right hand side of his tunic. To me he looked like the boss. I put on the desk my paper bag, which carried two bottles of soda and the loaves of bread which, from my point of view, should have been called envelopes -- the same loaves which were the cause of my guilt and which could earn me a night or nights in a police cell and a prison sentence.

"Good afternoon, Madam? Can I help you?" a middle aged officer asked. He opened the book which was in front of him and took out a pen. From what I saw of him, he expected me to give a report of an assault, theft, or loss

94

of property, but not a request to see a violent criminal.

"Yes, sir, I want to see two people, who I understand were arrested last night." That was exactly what Captain had advised me to say. I saw the officer take another book and after opening a page where there were names asked me: "Their names, please?"

"Jack Zollo and George Githenji." The mention of those two names made the officer open his mouth. At first I thought he usually opened his mouth wide before he talked but I realized later it was to help him see more clearly. His next move was to turn his head and look at the old officer with the stripes. The mouth was still wide open.

"What is it, officer?" the old man asked.

"This lady wants to see 'the two'." The old man looked at me closely. By being told 'the two', he had known whom I wanted. This reminded me of what Captain had told me (the best harvest the police have had in years). He came to me and asked: "Young lady, you want who and who?"

"Jack Zollo and George Githenji. Is it possible, sir?"

"Well..., yes. Who are they to you?"

"One is my husband, sir,"

They looked at each other, then looked at me from head to the shoe I was wearing. It was as if they couldn't believe I could get married, or I was stupid enough to get married to a gorrilla.

"Tell me, which of the two is your husband?"

"Must be Zollo, that young man has more surprises than his age," one of the officers volunteered to answer for me.

"Is that so?" asked the elderly man.

"Yes, sir," I said. They were looking at me with disbelief.

"What have you brought for them? There are things we do not allow. You know that?" By then he was reaching for the paper bag, my heart started its horse-racing. He opened the paper bag, took the sodas and put them on the desk. He took the bread too. He was doing this slowly as if he had no hurry in the world, and at the same time trying to make me feel that the law knew no money, smartness, youth, and whatever else we have in life.

My heart almost stopped when he took one bread and started examining it suspiciously. I started hoping that Captain had done a nice job. As he did so, he told one of the officers to bring out the two prisoners, one at a time. He then turned to me. "For how long have you been married?"

"About one year, sir."

"Have you got any children?"

"No, sir, we want to have a wedding first."

They again looked at each other, then at me. It was as if they were telling me that that was a daydream; that Jack was no longer mine but theirs, and would remain so for quite a long time. They then decided to chide me further.

"When are you planning to do that?"

"In two months' time, sir."

One of them laughed, then asked: "What do you do yourself? Had he opened some business for you?"

"No, I work with E.A.A."

"In town?"

"No, sir, at Embakasi."

"And what does your husband tell you he does?"

"He is a businessman. He has..." I stopped when they all started laughing, shaking their heads from side to side and showing signs of pity. But who cared? If they thought I didn't know my husband was a robber, they were the fools and not I, as they thought. When they had laughed enough, one of them, who to me seemed wild, said, *"Mama, tafuta mwingine. Huyu si wako tena. Ulimjua lini?"* I didn't answer that one. Although they at first seemed good to me,

96

they had gone a bit too far, under the circumstances. I looked at him and showed him clearly that I was not at all amused by his advice. Sensing my anger, he tried to sooth me. But it was already too late. I had come to hate them for being malicious. That was not the way they should have approached a lady whom they believed was about to lose her husband. Just then Zollo appeared.

My ever clean husband was shabby. I almost couldn't recognise him. His long hair was not combed and it had dust all over; he looked as if he hadn't used water for months, and hadn't slept a wink. His white shirt had dots of blood, which told me that he had tasted some beatings. He had no shoes, no belt... I mean he was really dirty and looked weary. I couldn't stand that sight. I bent my head and the next minute I was crying.

I looked up when he touched me. I was surprised to see he was smiling and ignoring the presence of his captors. He talked to me.

"Milly, do not do that. I'll soon be with you, if all goes well." The malicious officers looked at both of us. They seemed to tell me that Jack had told me yet another lie. But that too never bothered me. I had now known my husband enough. I knew he had ways and means of taking himself out of trouble. But this time it looked bad.

"Milly, do not stop going to work. Continue with everything you do just as if we were still together. Do you understand?" I nodded my head, I could not be able to talk.

"So far, do not do anything, just re..."

"Don't you want a lawyer?" The same wild officer intercepted. I saw Jack turn to him and say: "Mind your biz. Why don't you employ one for me? With the peanuts you earn?" I knew he was annoyed, but that did not stop me from wondering whether he had to be rude, even when he was a prisoner. But then, who can tell between the "cops and robbers". From my present knowledge, the two parties have very much in common. The wild cop only smiled. It was evident that they knew each other.

I got relieved when he was given the things I had brought without any hitch. He advised me that there was no need of my seeing Githenji, because all that was needed was to notify his wife of his whereabouts, a thing which Captain had already done. I left the place and went home.

Back at my thinking camp, I sat down, hiding my face in my hands as if in prayer. It was in this same place and in the same posture that I had cursed Jack and told myself that we were to part if he couldn't change. My thoughts were different this time. I started imagining life without him and saw that it would not do. I remembered the words of the wild officer, that Jack was no longer mine, and that I should find someone else, because he was sure that Jack was sunk. I started sweating in the palms of my hands. Would I ever see him again? Would all this mean prison sentence for my husband? What of the wedding we had always set aside so that we could do it when Jack wasn't on the run? Would he learn a lesson from this and let me marry him first thing when he came back? When would he come, anyway? I shared these troubles with him, but there was nothing I could do about it. With a criminal for a husband one had to learn the secret of patience, worry, loneliness, and the like.

He was taken to court three days later. I woke up early that day, as requested by Captain, who kept in touch all that time. I think I was the first person to arrive outside the Law Courts that day. Jack arrived at exactly 8.30 a.m. under a very heavy escort. By then a good number of peo-

98

ple had arrived. To see him handcuffed almost made me faint. There were four police officers leading him and Githenji, all armed with machineguns and about the same number behind them, who would turn this way and that, their guns pointed at those who were around as if they were expecting us to attempt a rescue. They were pushed inside the court.

Their charges were read at 9.30 a.m. It was at this time when I heard what I had expected. Among the lighter charges were a good number of car thefts. The robbery charges were, up to that time, three. The prosecutor also told the court that there were other similar charges to come and would the judge remand them at the maximum prison until the investigations were complete?

I looked at Jack and Githenji as all the charges were being read. They didn't seem to be worried. While the audience were pitying them and not believing that the smartly dressed young men in the dock were robbers, the two were smiling. As I saw the judge look at them through his dark glasses, I thought he didn't like them, and if he did, then he hated the charges. Jack turned his head to look at me; it was as if he was giving me a signal that he was about to leave, because a minute after, they were taken away. I got out of the court. In the corridor outside he talked to one of the guards who allowed me to talk with him. He told me that he was being taken to Kamiti prison remand and he would like me to try and visit him there the following day. They had been sent there for two weeks, after which they would be brought back to court.

"Two weeks without Jack?" I thought I was dreaming. I couldn't stomach the thought that I would stay for all those days without him. How would the house look like without him? I had gotten used to being with him and his absence would make me sick. What a life? Needless to say, I could not hold my tears back. No one could comfort me, not even my mother.

I was on my way home when a thought struck me. Probably there was someone who could give me a little comfort, a person Jack loved and the only one he ever talked about. It was this same woman who seemed to share Jack's bad days with him: his sister, Connie, the only member of Jack's family whom I had ever met. She was a likable young woman, married to a good husband who regarded Jack as his own brother. I called Connie's husband by phone and informed him of the misfortune that had befallen Jack and the next minute he was on his way to the telephone booth from where I was calling.

We drove to his wife's school where we discussed the matter. Both decided that we should consult a lawyer first thing the following day. At least when we parted after he had driven me home, I felt I had a pair to share with me the grief I carried.

I reported to work that afternoon. The boss had gone out of the country and at such times we would be in trouble with his Kikuyu deputy. You couldn't be on good terms with that one, unless you knew how to keep a date after 4.30 p.m. That is, if you happened to be good-looking (married or single) and if you wanted to keep your post. With Jack in prison, nothing mattered, not even the job. So when he wanted to know why I was absent in the morning and demanded that I report to his office around·4.15 p.m. with a written explanation, I left his office without a word. I was all ready to say goodbye to that office, which I had come to like.

I received a telephone message from mom at exactly 3.45 p.m. She wanted to see me urgently. With this and that in mind, I only took my handbag and called it a day. As I closed the door behind me, I said: "To hell with the deputy boss. He might just as well sack me." Miss Ironside heard the remark but only smiled. She had known all that was important to know about me.

Mom, it turned out, had problems somewhat similar to Jack's. Her illegal business of selling alcohol had landed her in police cells as well. It was a strange coincidence as she had been arrested on the very same day that Jack hadn't come home. Right then she was in prison, where she was already serving a sentence of three months, having been unable to pay the fine of Shs 1,000. They had been trying to get me on the phone for the past two days but to no avail. My young sister couldn't tell the difference between a box number and a telephone number. Luckily, in prison, mom managed to meet a person she could send and it was through him that I got the message.

I still had the money I was going to bank when the robbery occurred and I went straight to the Industrial Area G.K. prison and got mom out. She could see that I was in the worst mood, but she thought it was because of her two-day imprisonment. Well, it was a shock to hear of her imprisonment, but right then I had Jack's misfortune in mind. I had long decided not to let her know. I wasn't going to bring her into this. I wanted to suffer it out on my own. After all, I didn't see why I should give her some more worries when she had so much of her own.

Talk of ghosts and I'll give you Jack as an example. If he isn't a ghost, then there aren't any ghosts on earth. After parting with mom that evening in town, I went straight home. On opening the door, which had been locked, I found him seated on his usual sofa. I couldn't believe my eyes. I stood at the door, staring at the ghost, and of course, "using my mouth for my eyes" as he would say.

I moved when he talked. "Can you please close that door and lock it like never before?" I did that in a hurry, then went to him. I was weeping when he held me and pulled me towards him.

"I have made it, Milly. I have escaped and the town is hotter than hell right now. It will be hot for you too, so take care how you move about."

"Why me, dear? Why me?"

"Remember you came to see me at the police station and at the court? They already know you. One thing they cannot do is arrest you, but the moment they spot you, they'll follow you till you lead them here. And do not think it will be simple for you to spot them — that needs someone who has dealt with them for a time. They are only lucky that we can tell one from the way they walk. Do you understand what I mean?"

"I'll take care, dear, believe me, I will. I'd rather face anything than let them take you back."

"You do not have to tell me that, dear. I knew what I mean to you when you risked bringing me the message at the station. Anyway that is bygone. This now is the time to move on to another thing. I have much ahead of me and..."

"But darling, you must think deeply about this thing. I do not think we will make out of..." Well, none was giving the other time to talk. We were both confused, uncertain of what was next and how everything would end up. So the most advisable thing right then was to let things stay just as they were, and comfort each other in our usual way. We went to bed very late that night.

102

When trouble starts, it comes flying, landing on you from every direction. It was just a few months past when I had two of my best people hanging between freedom and jail. One being my mom and the other my husband. On coming out of prison mom had renewed her insistence on our wedding. She didn't give me peace; it was as if her two-day imprisonment had told her something might happen to her before she could witness the official marriage of her daughter.

This was a promise Jack and I had given her and time had passed, without any of us telling her how far we had gone with the arrangements. Jack was in a bad situation; not financially, but legally. The police did not give him a break and to remind him of the wedding and the nagging I got from mom would only be adding on him another load. It would be even, from my point of view, suicidal to attempt it. I didn't have the courage to tell mom that money was not the problem, neither was time and place, but that my husband was a fugitive in hiding. It was just as hard to tell her that the man she also liked and agreed to as being best suited for me was a confirmed criminal. So I had to carry the burdens of both sides alone and secretly.

Trouble attacked me from a different angle. A few months back I had visited a clinic to get rid of a 'third party' that had been forming in my uterus. Now I was pregnant again and I wasn't going to visit that clinic again even if it meant losing my job, which was most likely. I decided to take time before I let Jack know. All this time I didn't know what I was doing to myself. Instead, I thought I was making things move slowly and calmly before nature or fate intervened and sorted things out for the three of us. In the process I did not know that I was only hurting myself.

I did not even realize I was losing weight.

I felt brave and wise that I was able to endure and control intelligently the misfortune which had stuck itself right at the centre of our lives. It was only when Jack told me, that I realized I was doing great harm to myself. He had noticed the changes in me and so he called me and requested me to sit and have a talk with him. He said to me: "Milly, there is something bothering you. Let us talk and try to sort things out. You cannot go on like this for long." I thought for a few minutes then decided to tell him the whole truth. It was obvious that he was the only person whom I would share my problems with, so I gave him the whole story.

"Jack, I am pregnant. Mom is also nagging me about the wedding we had promised her. I have thought about this problem for a very long time and the more I think about it the more the solution eludes me. I have considered your situation and seeing that you have to stay indoors shows me that it is risky or rather impossible for the wedding to be carried out. And here is mom telling me about it everyday and as you know I cannot tell her the truth. I also have that shock which I got when you were arrested. I think it was at that time when I realized how easily I could lose you. I am worried, dear, about what would happen to me if you were imprisoned while I am expecting a baby. You must think about the whole issue seriously, dear. You have got away with it twice and each time you get away, you worsen the situation. The third time might be the worst if it happens to come."

' That tells me what is killing you. But, Milly, there are things that we shouldn't allow to worry us. I am glad that you are expecting a babe. It is high time we got company. But let us look at things from another angle. It is true that

104

I almost sank. There can also be a third, even a fourth
time, but must we allow these negative thoughts to plant
themselves in our minds? Why cross bridges we haven't
reached? My advice is that we stay the way we are right
now and hope for the best."

"What about my situation and my job? The moment
they realize I am in the family way, without certificates to
show that I am married, I'll lose the job. There is no question about that."

"That problem has come at the wrong time, Milly, and
I am afraid there isn't much I can do about it. I am even
thinking of absconding for a while. Things are real bad,
if I must tell you. However, I do not want you to worry
even a little about the whole thing. I'll see what I can do
about...I am not promising you much, anyway."

"Would you suggest abortion, before it is too late?"

"Why on earth should you do that? That's murder, Milly.
You'd feel guilty throughout your life."

I had already done it once. Now he had, instead of com-
forting me, made me feel like a murderer. The thought
that I had done this to enlighten the burden for him made
me start weeping. If he hadn't reminded me I would still
feel innocent, since much time had passed since I under-
went that sad experience. But I couldn't blame him. If I
had told him of the abortion in time, he probably wouldn't
have termed it as murder.

I felt like blowing up. My head started aching as it could
not hold all that I had. I pushed myself closer to Jack. If
there was anyone who could comfort me right then, it was
him. I had been missing his love badly since his manhunt
started. He seemed to have been very much carried away
by thoughts and had almost forgotten my presence. I held
him on the neck and whispered in his ear, "Jack, dear,

105

I want you, please. Take me inside, to the bed and destroy me completely. I want to feel you inside me, Jack. To reassure myself that you are still with me, that you still love me, that I mean something to you, please do so, Jack." I was serious because I was feeling so hot on him. His manner of caressing me always made me forget my problems and he seemed ignorant about the fact.

The way he whisked me from the seat reminded me of the very first day I came to this house. Jack was of my size, if not smaller, but from the way he handled me, I felt ten times smaller. It was hard to expect such strength from his physical size.

I threw my slippers away as he put me on the bed, my eyes closed, expecting to feel him any moment. He wasn't in a hurry, he let me sweat the sexual hunger alone, caressing me and leaving me hanging in the air. Then he came to me. Right inside as I wanted. By the time we were through, I had no worry in the world. All I needed was to listen to what he would suggest, provided he didn't mention about absconding and leaving me alone. I couldn't stomach that. What was wrong in staying indoors till every bit of fire was extinguished and the field got cool for him to move about?

Chapter 7

I reported on duty three days later. Miss Ironside came to me as soon as I sat behind my desk for she had news for me — bad news. She put a letter addressed to me on my desk, looking sad. I knew what it contained, and where it had come from. Though during the time I had worked with the firm I had never got such a letter, I knew that when the boss was not around, most of my workmates got such letters, giving them either a warning for being late and inefficient or interdicting them. We all thought negatively of this deputy boss. No one failed to note that he was a fool. He interdicted people as it pleased him and the following day, when the boss returned, they would be called back.

I opened the letter and read. It wasn't that hot. I was required to see him before I sat behind my desk. With all the problems in my mind, nothing seemed important to me any longer. Losing my job right then would have meant nothing to me. There was only one thing which would have made me go running into his office: that was if he had a way of getting Jack clear of trouble. I would have listened to him for hours without tiring. But now, I knew he only wanted to add more to the problems I already had and which were enough for me. I tore up the letter and got busy working on the heap of papers in my "IN" tray.

I looked up when I saw a shadow on the sheet I was typing. It was the deputy boss. We looked at each other for a good minute. He talked first. "Did you get my message?" Before I answered, I found myself thinking. I wanted to tell him that I wasn't interested and that the job no longer meant anything to me, and if he thought it would give him a chance of dating me, he had better think twice. I didn't tell him anything; the answer I gave him was to look at the wastepaper basket beside me, where I had thrown the letter I had torn up. He followed my eyes and saw it. As if he couldn't believe his eyes, he passed by me and picked it up. Shaking his head in disbelief, he went away. I thanked God I had done that. That was the last day he ever talked to me. It was a very risky gamble to take, but it worked. I guess, having stayed with criminals for such a long time had turned me into a hard nut. After all, I wasn't sure I was going to work with them for more than three months, now that I was pregnant and still not legally married.

My husband was, up to that time, still indoors. He never went out, even during the night. But the more the days passed by, the more he considered absconding. Two more weeks indoors made him decided.

I listened to him, tears flowing from my eyes incessantly. I could not believe I was listening to the very person I knew. I couldn't believe he was really planning to leave me and go. But I could understand. My worry was: where would he go to? Who would take care of him when he was away? And for how long would he be away? Would he find other women and forget about me completely? That last one almost made me faint. I was of the jealous type; I never ever liked to even think of sharing him with anybody else on this earth. Luckily, I trusted him. He never failed me when I needed him and that was another good aspect of the life he had introduced me to.

He left on a Sunday at around 3.30 a.m. We had spent the weekend together, all days and nights talking. He convinced me that if he didn't go, then I would lose him

108

forever. He had so many criminal charges awaiting that he believed being sent behind bars for less than thirty years would be a favour done to him by the judge. Having known a few of them, I had no doubts in me that it was the truth.

"I'll miss you, Milly. The blame of whatever is going to happen is mine. I owe you an endless apology for leading you to a miserable life. Please remain loyal till I come back. Have no worry at all about me, I know my way wherever I find myself. If there is anyone you should worry about, let it be yourself. Do things as if we were still together. Try to imagine me beside you always. But please, don't let the imagination carry you to the extent of comparing me with another man.

"That, dear, might bring two important lives to a sad end." I was listening because those were the last words I expected to hear from him, probably for years, till we would meet again. But I could not help weeping. Since I met this man, I guess I had cried and wept more times than when I was a baby, only, it was because of this thing the world felt better to name "LOVE". I wished it never existed.

"I promise to be faithful, dear! I mean ... there is no need for you to tell me. I just can't imagine having someone else. It even hurts me to hear you tell me that. How can you tell me, dear? Is that the amount of trust you have in me?" I realised from his silence that I was hurting him, so I cut that stuff. Instead I decided to give him the same tablet to swallow.

"Jack, I have known you for long. I have always trusted you. Please, don't kill the trust when you go, just because I am not with you. You know you like women, Jack, I know it too, but I have never caught you red-handed and so I have no suspicions that you move with them when you are away from me. But I wouldn't like to imagine you in bed

with another woman. I swear, I would kill the two of you.
I swear that would be the last..."

"Please do not go over that again. I wouldn't touch
anyone, apart from you. Not even the last one, if this world
went on fire and left the two of us only." It was a lie, I
knew and believed it was. But like a fool, it consoled me
as usual.

His case was simple. He didn't have much to worry about
because he had left some "bodyguards" behind. I stood
at the window early that morning as he ignited the "company car" and left for an unknown destination.

I was used to being with a husband. It was a bad experience to stay without one for several months. All the
time I imagined he was lying beside me, while the truth
was that he wasn't. The worst came when I imagined him
with another woman in bed. Sleep would go out through
the window and the following morning I would wake up
late.

At this time, I happened to be taking care of some
children for a maternal relative. I had to cook for them
and take them to school, since they were unfamiliar with
the city. This sometimes caused me to miss the company
transport and subsequently arrive late for work, till one
day the boss himself had to summon me to his office.

I applied for leave when I realized I was about to spoil
my record with the boss. I hadn't gone on leave for a long
time, so I was granted two months. This was enough time
to train the children to go by themselves to school and come
back home. The good thing was that they weren't very
young.

I wouldn't remember how I got the idea of aborting
again. Although I had firmly decided not to abort this time,

110

the circumstances were not favourable for my pregnancy.

Firstly, I had to keep on seeing my mother who would soon notice that I was pregnant and regard me as being disobedient and even immoral, since we had not met her demand for a lawful marriage. Secondly, she would soon notice that Jack was missing and I would have a difficult time explaining to her his whereabouts, which I actually did not know. She was likely to take it that Jack had jilted me, and she would be so disappointed. And, to make matters worse, I was likely to lose my job in a few months' time. I argued that I could always get another baby when the two of us were reunited. So I visited my doctor early enough and, for the second time, our son, or daughter, was gotten rid of. But as Jack would put it, I had committed a second murder.

Life wasn't as bad as I had anticipated. However, in the beginning I experienced some hard times. I had enough money to push me for years, even without my salary, but money is not all that counts. I wanted my husband with me. But as months went by I began to get used to it. Jack's younger brother, who resembled him a lot, had at this point moved into the house to keep me company. It was nice to look at him and remember my husband. He looked so much like Jack that I at times tended to think that he was our son. But with the knowledge that he wasn't, I got a feeling every now and then that the boy actually belonged to the woman Jack loved before he met me. How was I to know the truth? Asking my husband would just be useless.

At times, I was glad of all that had happened, especially when I thought that on coming back, Jack would have learnt a lesson. I did not expect him to do anything that would force him to leave his own country ever again. On the other hand, I had seen how staying indoors had hurt him, how it had given him tensions. It was unthinkable that he would be induced by anything to go back to it. I had also learned from Captain, who kept on seeing us, that most of the members of their gang had died and those whom Captain regarded as being lucky had been sentenced to life imprisonment. Within the same month that Captain had given me this news, he was sent in for one year. I had no doubt that Jack would learn a lesson from all this.

Though Jack didn't take one year, I felt like I had missed him for ten. I went home that day as usual, straight from work. When I stepped out of the company car, which normally took me as far as the gate, I met the maid. She didn't know who Jack was, as I had hired her a month after Jack had left. She stopped when she saw me, making me think she was on to some mischief. When she gave me the news of a visitor the children referred to as Uncle Jack, I think she made a mad woman of me. I ran as if I had seen death behind me. She came after me, not certain that there wasn't danger around. By the time she reached the door, I was already on Jack.

It was like opening a new chapter of an interesting novel. All the miseries, loneliness, troubles, thoughts, queer dreams, and other horrible things which used to haunt me, ended that minute, when I was eating him alive on the ground. The maid saw what was happening and left. The children forgot to go and play outside with their friends and decided to see this free film which would normally have been censored "for adults only". But I wasn't with them, nor did their presence mean anything to me. There was only me and Jack, as far as I was concerned.

I guess he was expecting that to happen, for he didn't

112

stop me. He let me amuse myself to my satisfaction. When I got my breath back, I let him go, and it was only then that I was able to stand and admire him. I wanted to size him up and see what he had been doing with himself. From various things, I felt I could easily detect the small sins I believed he must have committed.

"I missed you for all those years, Jack. Oh God ... you look nice! That place was good for you." I wasn't giving him time to tell me anything. It was as if it was I who had gone away. "Tell me, Jack, did you miss me much? Tell me so."

"Well..."

"Oh don't tell me you didn't. How dare you hesitate. Who is that who kept you so busy that you had to forget me? Who is that thief?" I noticed that he got annoyed, when I called her a thief. I was getting him step by step.

"You call her a thief. You call..."

Guilty after all. I had caught him. There was someone he could not stand being referred to as a thief. And yet she must have been. Jack belonged to me and not her.

The fact that I had to start weeping within minutes of our reunion took me back to the time before he left and the troubles he got me into. How could he admit having had an affair with someone else while I was dying for him back at home?

It was good to have Jack home; better to hear him swear he would never involve himself in crime again, and best to hear that we would soon wed. I visited mom and gave her the good news. Her joy upon hearing that, told me she had been very anxious to see us marry officially. Within the same week of hearing the news, she made a visit to Jack's parents to cement the relationship forever. Jack's parents couldn't believe it. I think they doubted their son could

113

come to a stage where he would need a wife. They commended me for what they termed as "dragging Jack to Heaven".

I was able to work pefectly and the record with my boss, which I had almost blemished, got to normal. Everything in our self-contained life became better than ever before. Jack had realized that I had aborted for the second time, since he didn't meet a son as he was expecting when he came back from exile. I remember his first question was what we got from the bulging belly he had left me with. Although he outrightly called it murder, he understood the circumstances which had forced me to do that. This was one of the many things that I liked him for. He was always understanding and ready to accept reality.

I believed our wedding would go ahead when Jack started getting busy. He took me to a tailor who was to make the wedding dresses. He made the most necessary arrangements, meaning that all that remained was to name the big day. I relaxed; forgot all the miserable days I had encountered during his days of crime, and I started gaining weight; feeling strong and more responsible for the future family.

I did not need to remind Jack of the past days, when we lived in great fear, and the law was our number one enemy. He kept on talking of how foolish he had been to have gone that far. He knew he was only very lucky to have survived his criminal days. That told me everything. His regrets meant a lot to me; it meant a lot to his life and all those who liked him. It was the only thing which would be able to build our future.

Hail the day when a confirmed criminal will give up his arms and ammunitions and call it quits with crime. To my knowledge, that day will never come. Here was Jack, who had sworn never to hold a gun again; Jack, who assured me that the day he ever would hold it again would be when he handed it over to the law, or when he would be throwing it away. He was sure I knew where he kept it. What made me suspicious was that he removed it and hid it somewhere else. I came by it accidentally. The rounds of ammunition were still intact, although they were no longer anywhere near our house, as far as he was concerned. I played dumb again to see what he would do. It was useless to advise him to throw it away before he chose to do so, for I knew that he would still have it back if he felt like it.

It didn't take long before I read in the newspapers of another bank robbery. The day in question, Jack had lied to me that he would visit his parents at home for further arrangements towards the wedding. When he came back the following day, it was to prepare himself for consulting a private doctor, as his head had nearly stopped a bullet. He had a wound in the head where a bullet had grazed him, a wound which made him sleepless and forced him to resume staying indoors again; back to the same boredom of spending days lying on the sofa set, smoking non-stop and eating almost nothing for days. He couldn't get words to explain what had happened; why he had gone back to the dark days after swearing he wouldn't. Asking him was as useless as buying him The Holy Bible. He would only show me his good smile and tell me to try and forget it. I had no option but to do exactly that. What angered me was the fact that he failed to realize he hurt me terribly when I thought of the whole issue. Would it be that he got a kick from doing such evils? He never looked like a criminal; you could easily have mistaken him for a smart preacher.

I thought the proverbial maximum "forty days" said to be for a thief at large were at hand. He had stayed indoors long enough and had decided to see what was going on around town. The next thing I heard about him was that he was in the hands of the law; this time never to make his witty breaks. I was on duty when I received the bad news. I felt and saw the end of my beloved husband. This was the time when I critically questioned the meaning of my life. Why did I have to be so unlucky as to lose the one who was really mine? Why me of all people? What had I done to God to deserve the punishment?

I visited him at the police station the following day. He was still mine and I wasn't going to leave him for the wolves; I was going to stick to him till he realized he had messed me up and regretted it the rest of his life. I loved to see him weep. I visited him with our unborn still in me, a son he would never hold and love till the law was through with him. I knew it would hurt him, for he was looking forward to hearing himself being addressed as "Father" and to feel being a father to a son whose mother I was sure he loved. But the tears were not his alone. We shared problems to the very end. We would both start weeping when our eyes met through the bars which prevented us from shaking hands; from the kisses we knew too well; from the caresses we so much liked and from the jokes, fun and the whispers in the ears. All these were buried memories, dreams that were shattered by the same invisible cloud which shattered the days we made love. All that was left were imaginations and suffering; the loss of learning what might have been, had we succeeded.

I visited the court on the judgment day. I wasn't alone; mom was with me too, weeping more than I was. At times,

I remembered those days in the very beginning when we discussed my husband-to-be. How I hated those days when I was forced to protect him from my mom's true accusations; the days we went to see him come to court in handcuffs under a heavy guard looking beaten up, those same days when we stayed till we saw him ushered back into the Black Maria, and the police cars follow behind him their sirens wailing, announcing there was a dangerous person whom the law had picked out from the good ones. They are days I'll live to remember and hate. But that had to pass.

Amongst those who attended his trial, I guess I was the only one who could clearly see his end. I had stayed with him longest. I knew he wasn't being framed; I had seen and spent much of the money he had robbed, because I loved him and could not refuse spending it. It was this time when he was going to pay for all that. I too was going to pay for it by losing him whom I loved; by witnessing a great shame; by carrying a baby whose dad it would never see and know; by trying to explain why he didn't have a dad like the other children, and many other things.

But funny enough, I never regretted meeting him. He was mine, and the only one I could bring myself to love. I never saw beyond him. And I wasn't wrong: he was the only one whose love would be termed genuine, that is, as far as I was concerned. The worst experience was this day, the day, if I must repeat, of judgment. I remember the police officer who approached me and asked me if I was Milly. I gladly told him I was. By then all I had in mind was that Jack had probably thought of a way which would save him, such as asking me to bring a gun to the law-courts so that he could use it to escape. I swear I would have done it. It would not have been the first day for me to carry it

117

in my handbag. I would have done it; I would have done worse than that if it meant having him back to myself. But what he brought to me was the worst thing I ever saw.

The policeman handed a letter to me. I took it and went to the "Ladies" to see what it contained. That was before the case opened for the first time. I opened the envelope and read;

Dear Milly,

It must sound crazy to say that I am a born criminal. But through what we both have undergone, we would be inclined to believe this. You know, as much as I do, that I have many times sworn never to involve myself in crime but to no avail. I have tried to keep a low profile so that I may fit into society, without any success. All of these attempts ended up in flames. I always knew I was "bad news". I knew I was doing the wrong thing. But something kept pulling me to the same thing. I had no need for big money, Milly, and you know it. What did I ever do with whatever I got, anyway? Boozing? Would you call that an achievement? That was madness. I think what was in my mind was adventure; a thing I sought in the wrong way.

I know what I have done with your life: I have ruined it. Please forgive me for this. I know I was the first man in your life, which makes me feel even more guilty. But it is too late. Please let me not be the last. Probably from the second lover, you'll learn more and your future will no longer be at stake. Believe me dear, I feel very sorry about the whole issue, especially the shame I have caused you. Your luck, Milly, lies somewhere else, not anywhere near me. With me, only

118

*the devil has chances of luck, and you know where
the devil will always lead you.*

*Where I am going is where we pay all the evils we
have done. I deserve it, Milly. Whatever judgement
I'll get will be what I deserve. Please look at the judge
with a kind eye, as he passes my sentence. If he gives
me less than thirty years, rest assured that he loves
me. It will be a great favour. What would you expect a violent robber like me to get? A gold medal?
That would be unthinkable. But it is just too bad,
Milly, that this had to happen when I had realized
I was following the wrong track. Believe me, I swear,
the last bank I hit would have been my last. My last
adventure had come to an end.*

*The greatest loss I'll live to remember is you. To
me, you are the first and last. Quoting the Bible you
love, "Alfa and Omega". These words were from the
mouth of Jesus Christ, whom you believe is your
saviour. I am sure he hasn't deserted you up to now.
You'd be the last person he'd desert. But forgive me
to say that this was written: You were not meant for
me, Milly. NEVER. Otherwise, why should this happen just when I am ready to give up everything for
your sake? The Kikuyu elders said, "Wendo munene
ndukinyaga," (Great love does not end up well). What
would you say about that? Isn't that proved true from
what the two of us have witnessed? I loved you, and
you know it. I too know you've always loved me. You
do, up to this moment when I am about to go behind
bars for forty years.*

*Milly, it is a pity that you'll always love me. Could
you please be kind enough to break the love, for your
own sake? Give it to the second lover. I promise not*

to be jealous; only do not, under whatever circumstances let me know. That alone would kill me. But I insist you do it. Find another one from the millions I am leaving you with. Please do. I will always..."

I found it hard to complete reading that letter. It was so hurting that I cried out loudly from where I was — in the "Ladies", if you know what I mean. I wish I understood what he was telling me. The letter told me much that I didn't know. But what good would it do to me when I knew it was the last? And that reminds me also that it was the first.

I left the "Ladies" and went to the court-room. Most of the witnesses had given their testimonies and what now remained was the judge's word. I looked at him kindly, as requested by my husband. It had occurred to me that even criminals bore no hatred for those who sent them behind bars. I saw the judge take out his specs to size my husband up. I thought that if I wasn't wrong, he liked Jack Zollo. If not so, he pitied him. It was as if he knew the young man had driven himself to something horrible, ignorantly. He called him and asked him whether he had anything to say in mitigation. Jack stood up and looked at me. The sight of his eyes made me start weeping. I had made sure I didn't go back to sit next to my mom. It would have been very bad. Instead, I had gone and sat between Jack's sister, Connie, and his mother. I wanted them to know they were not in the suffering alone. That there was someone else who was feeling the pains as much as they did. But, I was different; I knew much more about their brother and son than they did, and also the fact that he was under no circumstances going to get away with it.

"Your honour…," Jack mitigated. "… this is entirely for you to decide. I have heard as much as you have. But I have one advantage over you: I know the truth. But what I have might not interest you. I'll be satisfied with your judgment."

Needless to say, I heard my husband being convicted to twenty years imprisonment. To Jack, it was a favour, but to me, it was the end of the greatest love I have ever known. I screamed. But what good would that do? Jack was whisked away and sent to prison. But I remember he was smiling. Probably because the judge had done him a favour, or because he had been stinking crazy, all along. I mean, how could someone smile after being convicted to twenty years' imprisonment? I hung around to witness him being ushered into the Black Maria to go and start his long stretch. For me, his lover, it was endless tears.

Chapter 8

It was a hard experience watching all my love go down the drain. People stared at me, not believing I was the wife, or probably pitying me for what lay ahead for me. I was feeling so bad that if it wasn't for mom, who came and held me, I would have found myself on the floor, for I was fainting. When I regained consciousness, I was lying under a tree. There were people beside me, whom I could not recognize at once. It surprised me to realize that these people were my mom, Jack's mom and sister, a few friends and relatives. I didn't talk to any one of them. What could I have told them, anyway, and they had witnessed everything for themselves? They had their lovers around; mine had been whisked to a land of confinement. I picked my handbag, hung it on my shoulder and left. I wanted to have time alone, time to condemn the devil who had done all this to me, to think how I would manage a life without the one I loved; to try and imagine I was in his hands, my head on his chest as it used to be; to imagine the caressings he very well knew how to perform, and...to start my endless tears.

Life was never the same any longer. Nothing would give me consolation in the coming years. I think the only days I would say were better were those when I went to see him in prison. I would weep on seeing how he was reduced to zero. But on coming back home I'd feel him. My imagination of our past at such times would make sense. All I hated was to hear him tell me to find another man. Twenty years wasn't long enough to make him an old man. I wasn't twenty yet and I felt there was hope that my luck didn't lie anywhere near him. Probably it could be that he said it from shame, or to comfort me. But from whichever angle I observed things, I saw him as my only future. I wanted him to live in my memory and I was glad I was able to keep him with me even in his absence.

Years passed by and I continued visiting him in prison. I would talk to a prison officer and persuade him to smuggle in some money for him, because I had learned that he needed it. He had never asked me for money but I could guess it was because he wanted me to keep whatever I earned; he claimed I needed every penny I earned, now that I had no one else to support me and I had a child.

But I wanted him to be happy and to know that I was up to that time with him in memory. I would give the officer one hundred shillings for himself and two hundred for my husband; he would send a message to tell me he had got the money and that I should not do it again. "If I am caught with the money, dear, it will be the end of me," he would say. "Money is illegal in prison, dear, it is a crime to be in possession of it." The same warden he would send to bring the letter to me would be having another letter for a friend of his, or for his sister, Connie. The letters would be demanding money from them. Jack was a mysterious person and up to that time, prison seemed not to have changed him any bit.

I took his son to visit him, twice. When the baby was two years and when he was eight. The boy, who reminded me of his father every time I looked at him, was so much like Jack. He had adopted his father's manner of asking questions, which stung like a bee. There were times he wanted to know why he was a son of a woman while all his classmates were sons and daughters of men.

"Mum, don't I have a dad?" He was eight then and in Standard II.

"Why do you ask, son?"

"Why do I have to call myself Zollo Nyambiu. Weren't you married when you begot me?"

"My son, every child in this world has his dad. Some were unfortunate, because their fathers died from car accidents, others drowned in rivers during heavy rains, and others died in hospitals."

"But they still refer themselves as their fathers' sons, dead or alive. What happened to my father? Please tell me, mum. You weren't married, then?"

This gave me shame, especially when it came from my son.

"I was married, son, and I am still married."

"To my dad?"

"Yes, son, to your dad."

"And where is he? Why doesn't he come to visit us or stay with us?"

"But he comes and goes, son. You have seen him here many times."

"That is a lie. That man who comes here can't be my dad. Why is he so black and I am so brown? I was told by Aunt that he isn't my father. That is why I do not use his name." He was tormenting me, ignorantly, and there was nothing I could do about it. The boy seemed too clever for his age. I had no doubt that someone had told him the truth. But that was not all: he too had some intelligence that I hadn't seen in most children. I had to tell him the truth.

"Son, your dad is in prison. Do you know what prison is?"

"I think I do. What does he do there?"

"Just staying and being trained."

124

"To become a teacher like you?"

"No. To become something else. A carpenter, a cobbler, a tailor or a mechanic. It is for him to decide what he will be when he comes out."

"When will he come?"

"Not soon, son. But he will come and join us."

"And why don't we visit him in college?"

"Not college, son, prison. You said you know what prison is."

"Yes, when do we visit him in prison? Mom, I must see dad. Please..."

I had to make arrangements and take him there. He did not give me rest. Every morning he made sure he reminded me of the visit as I took him to school. I had long left East African Airways and joined teaching. This was arranged by Jack's mother, who up to that time took care of me. She had taken me up to the college and for two years she stayed with her grandson. Jack did not know of it; we had decided to keep it to ourselves. My mom had no objection. She liked Jack's mother and said whatever was decided between the two of us had her whole approval. That way, life was made easy for me.

In February, 1979, I told my son we would go to visit his father in prison. That night he did not sleep. I woke up early in the morning and went to his bedroom. The boy wasn't there. I thought he had gone to the toilet so I went to the tableroom. He was there. He had taken a bath and changed. I was surprised, I looked at the wall clock and saw it was 6.30 a.m.

"Son, why did you have to wake up so early? It is cold in the morning."

"Mom, I am eager to see my dad. I couldn't sleep. Let's go. You said we would go early." In one hour, I was ready.

We reached Naivasha town at around 8.30 a.m. The boy didn't see much on the journey, as he was aleep. The dirt road to the prison was over two kilometres. When I was alone, I normally went on foot when I knew I was too early. This time I hired a taxi.

Jack was brought to the visitors' room at 9.30 a.m. While we waited, his son kept nagging me. He would go to the prison officers passing by and enquire why his dad had taken so long. He even asked one officer whether his father wore such uniform.

He was disappointed to realize that he wasn't going to shake hands with his father but instead talk with him on the phone, looking at him through glass. But it was a very clear vision.

"Here comes your father now. See, he is a short man, as I told you," I said when Jack appeared.

"Isn't he coming here, mom?"

"No. You'll talk to him on that phone. Go closer." He started weeping. I was surprised; I had not seen him weep for over three years. I went and took the phone.

"Why did you have to come with him? What do you want him to know, so that he could hate me?" He sounded angry. It was ridiculous that that was the welcome he gave me. I wasn't surprised; I expected that from Jack. Not that he wasn't grateful of my visits. It was only that he was concerned, seeing that my journeys cost me so much in fare and time. But he failed to realize that in trying to be that good, he was hurting me, as I had as much concern for him as he had for me. This, however, was the last visit I ever made.

"Ask your son that question. He will tell you. Do you know how much and for how long I have resisted?"

"What do you think I feel seeing his tears. Do you..."

126

"Jack, will you never learn to be soft. I find it fair to warn you that your son is very intelligent. So try to act like a good father. You'll talk with him and find out for yourself."

All the time we were talking, his eyes were on his son. I could sense that he was overjoyed to see him and probably noticed their resemblance. "Give him the phone. He has wept enough." I turned to Zollo Junior. "Here son, talk to your dad. If you continue weeping, he will dislike you and will never come to join us. Take care." He took the phone.

"Hello, son. How are you?" the father called. The smile on his face reminded me of everything. I hadn't seen it any time I visited him. It probably had been reserved for the son.

"Dad, when are you coming?"

"Very soon, when I know you are good to your mum, I'll come."

"Am good to her, dad. I told her I wanted to see you. I knew that black man who comes home wasn't my dad. I am happy to see you. Can you come with us? Isn't your training over?"

"Not yet, son." He was now looking at me. The son had talked of another man.

"I don't like the clothes you are wearing, dad. They look bad."

At least he was sweating it out. I enjoyed every minute of it. If there was anyone who could change him, it was his own son. I could see how much bothered he was as the son pestered him with questions I, for one, couldn't answer. The warders with us were laughing, admiring the intelligence of the young boy who sounded doubtful any time he was given a dissatisfactory answer. But his father was

127

another one who wasn't easily outsmarted. They made a good pair. We all marvelled at the happiness between the father and son.

As for me, I went to my usual practice: weeping as the buried memories of my most beloved man came back. They talked for the maximum time, fifteen minutes. Each time the warder went for the phone the son would protest, almost violently. It was only when his father was forced to put the receiver down that the son reluctantly banged his also. We went out, but not before the son saw him disappear. The son had known the father, and the father likewise. The debt now was on the father. Would that change him? I wondered.

I got the second child after nine years. Jack's son was approaching his tenth birthday. I felt like having badly offended Jack. I could not visit him again, I couldn't stand his eyes looking at me with a baby that wasn't his. I didn't want him to question me either, which I was sure he would. I found it best to stay away from him, because I too didn't like what I had done. But I was still single and longing for him.

Chapter 9

It was last year when I saw the ghost again. The same ghost I had once seen when I sat in the living room praying for him; praying that the demons he had be sent to the pigs. This time, the ghost was not seated where I had seen it the last time. It stood at the door, fifteen years since the law parted us, six years since I last saw him, when I visited him in prison with his son.

When I answered a knock at the door, he was standing there, looking exactly as I knew him a decade and half ago. I couldn't believe my eyes. I believed I was dreaming. It was when he talked that my eyes appreciated the picture and the truth that it was Jack standing there.

"Hi, Milly. Can I come in?" I stood aside. I didn't know what to do. Something warned me not to take him in my hands the way I used to. I longed to do it but I wasn't sure he felt the same about it. It was a long time since we were so close, yet it felt as if the period was shorter than the time he had absconded when the town was hot for him.

He moved straight in and took a seat. From there, he looked at the ceiling first, he wasn't talking but seemed to be deep in thought. He then stood up to look at the pictures I had on the wall. They were many and there were a few of me and him in the good old days. He stared at each picture for minutes before he moved to the next. I could detect some pains in him. Then the baby started crying from the bedroom. I saw him turn to look at me, his face sad and seeming to criticise my deeds. I looked away from him and went to attend to the girl. She was three then. Jack hadn't talked up to now. Inside the bedroom,

I started it all over again, weeping. He had reminded me of so many things just by looking at him. I hated myself for not being patient enough. At times I felt I should blame him for all that. He had insisted that I find someone else, as he too didn't expect to see the outside of the prison walls that soon. It really seemed soon because that was not when I expected him. He must have left several years before his time. Or had he broken out of jail? It was hard to know with Jack.

I went back to the living room, holding the child. He had seen enough of the pictures and was now seated on the sofa, his eye closed as if in prayers. He opened them when I took a seat opposite him. He took a minute admiring the baby in my hands, then opened up.

"How have you been doing, Milly?" That name which had gone to jail with him came back. No one else called me by that name, because I never liked it. It reminded me of my bitter experiences.

"I have been doing fairly well."

"Same with me. You haven't changed much."

"Thank you." What else could I say.

"Thank you, for?" He had started it all over again. Making me feel young, like the good old days when we met and I couldn't get words to tell him or to explain why I thanked him. I kept quite to await his next move.

"Where is the father?" He gestured, indicating the child.

"Just within town."

"Are you married?"

"No."

"What are you waiting for?"

"Please, Jack, your questions are too direct and I feel unable to be as direct."

"So, how would you like me to put them? You know I

130

don't like beating about the bush. When are you marrying?"

"When God wishes, Jack. I left everything to God."

"You like your husband?" I kept quiet for a while. I wasn't sure what he was driving at, and I was afraid of hurting him.

"Milly, I am not asking you that question because there is something I want you to do about it. I want to know that you are happy. That you love your husband, because if you do not, life will never be kind to you. You know, I believe I was the wrong person for you. I mean, a man like me would never make a good husband. I want you to be happy..."

"I am happy, Jack. Please do not remind me of yourself. It would only hurt me. You shouldn't talk that way of yourself. You have always been good, very kind to me, and you have the concern of a good husband. There is only one thing which spoils you, Jack. You should do something about it."

"What is that?"

I hesitated. I was not decided on whether to tell him straightaway or not. It felt like he wasn't the person I once knew; the person I called my husband. I didn't know how much prison had changed him; for better or for worse. But that feeling was in me. He wasn't the same. He was talking with me freely, the humorous touch he always had was up to now still with him. But there was some bitterness in his voice; face, and even his smile looked phony to me.

There was one thing that I could not mistake: he was still in love, just as I was. I didn't have to show him that his comeback had meant a lot to me. But I had to be loyal to the new man I already had. We weren't married, but were planning to do so soon. I was happy, anyway, that

131

this had to happen in Jack's presence. Our marriage would have reminded me of Jack and his terrible situation, and that would have brought a lot of difference.

I looked at him to see if there was anything I could read from his face before I told him what I had always wanted to tell him. Probably he already had decided to do it on his own. But I had to tell him, so that he might know that he wasn't in it alone. He didn't wait; he seemed to sense I feared to tell him the wrong thing.

"You were telling me of that thing which spoils me. What is it?"

"Jack, I am finding it hard to tell you. You know I do not have that freedom I used to have on you. I must think, before..."

"That's being foolish, Milly. You can't say that to me. I can stand and go, and forget I ever had you in life. But if you feel you have welcomed me, I feel the same about you."

"Jack, have you changed? Have you given yourself time to think about your future?"

"You want to know of the truth? A frank answer?"

"Of course, otherwise I shouldn't know at all."

"Anyone who thinks of the future is a dreamer. Whoever can..."

"Please, Jack, don't say that. It is for each of us to plan this future through deeds and through arrangements, knowing what is good for you and what isn't. This is the only way which will make your dreams of a good future come true."

"Look here, Milly, there you are seated and nursing a babe which doesn't belong to me. I thought my future was to live with you forever. I planned it and did everything to build our future. Now, tell me, will you ever be my wife as we thought? Will you ever feel me beside your bed? How many times did you tell me we would do this and that in future when we got married? There is nothing like the future people talk about. What is of great importance is to have the fun for today. And of course, if you are married with your children, you..."

"You are no longer the same, Jack. Things will never be the same either." I looked at him. There was something very wrong with him. Prison had changed him. It had given him new principles, different from those he had before.

"So I am no longer the same. What of you? Are you the same?" I wasn't, but I wasn't going to tell him so. I wished he would change the subject and let us, for a while, remind ourselves of the happy days we used to have. He talked again.

"You are the same Milly. Good looking and lovable. But you are guilty. You didn't expect me to be back. You thought I would die in prison. Isn't that so? I didn't die. I made it as I have always done..."

I ignored whatever he was saying and asked: "When did you come?"

"Two months ago. I was pardoned, somehow, good luck for me. I did not expect pardon. I still had some more six years to serve."

"Did you have to take that long before seeing me? Two months?"

"I had to trace you. You gave up visiting me years ago. But now I know why." He looked at the child and I knew what he meant.

133

"You told me to find another man. You never once encouraged me to have hope on you. Every time I came, you insisted I shouldn't, and that I find myself a man among the millions I was with. I did it."

He smiled bitterly and I knew he would insult me. He did. "So you went out looking for a man who'd suit you? You didn't wait for them to come to you? It must have given you a hard time, Milly. Why did you have to do that? Didn't it ever occur to you that I still needed you?"

The child I was holding slept and I took her to bed. When I came back, he called me to his seat. I stood there, not knowing what to do. I did not want to disappoint him, yet I did not want to wrong my new fiancé. He didn't share the house with me. This was my school house, but he used to visit me every weekend.

I knew I could not resist Jack, if he started working on me. I still loved him, but these were not the old days.

"Are you coming here to sit with me or not, Milly?"

"I want to prepare something for you. We will talk..."

"Come here, forget about everything else first," he commanded.

I had never heard him talk that way. But I wasn't afraid of him. One thing I knew for certain was that Jack would never turn into a rapist, nor a murderer, but his love was dangerous.

I looked at him, still standing where I was and confused. I considered my dilemma: having two husbands, both of whom I loved. But Jack's love had no comparison. I felt his stare pulling me. That had happened some years back. Slowly, I went and sat next to him.

His arm on my shoulders made me shiver. I started feeling some warmth in my blood. I felt sweat gathering up. I was doing the wrong thing and I could not help it.

134

"Milly," he called. "I have loved you all that time. I have dreamt of you always. Your memories helped me to lead a clean life in prison. But as you said, I am not the same as I used to be. I cannot be loved any longer. Especially by you. I know..."

"But I still love you, Jack, I swear I do." I was nearly weeping. My love for him had come back in storms, making my body shake. I found myself pushing closer to him and, as always, I rested my head on his chest, feeling protected.

"Say that again, Milly."

"What?"

"That you still love me."

"But I am honest, Jack I swear I do." I felt as if I was drunk. It was then that his breath told me he was drunk.

"You love your husband too. You said you do. Isn't that rather odd?"

"But it is only because I have to stay with him."

He didn't talk more at the moment. He kept silent, caressing me as he used to. He hadn't forgotten any bit of it. The Christian fiancé I had seemed to fear me. There was no doubt about that. Whenever I wasn't in the mood for his company, I told him so, and he went straight home, without arguing. That had never happened between me and Jack; he was irresistible.

He turned my head and kissed me. His alcoholic breath was wonderful. I got hold of his neck and pulled him to me. I was violent and almost hurt him. He didn't resist, he let me amuse myself while he continued caressing me. It was as if I was in dreamland.

The door opened and our son entered. He had been away to visit his grandmother in Bahati. We didn't move from our position; I for one felt rudely interrupted. Then Jack

135

pushed me away gently.

The son recognized his father. He dropped the paper bag in his hands and rushed forward calling out:

"Dad, you have come home at last? I missed you." The father stood to take him. They were going to be of the same height. The boy was fourteen years then and was growing physically strong, and tall.

"Dad, will you go away again?" They had now dismissed me.

"I am afraid so, my son?"

"Why? Back to prison?"

"No. Back to where I stay." The son looked at me, then back at his father. I felt like crying.

"But dad, must you go?"

"Yes son. I have to go. This is your mother's home, not mine."

"But you can stay with us here. Please, dad, do not go."

I hid my head between my hands and started to pray for myself; my son and his father, and my fiancé. I wished this had not happened. The boy loved his father so much that he had completely refused to accept my fiancé as his father. We were worried about it, but there was nothing we could do. The fiancé understood and ignored the boy's daily accusations that he wasn't his true father. But we never failed to wonder when this boy's attitude would change. Like father like son; perhaps he wasn't going to change.

I prayed for a long time. I was glad they did not interrupt me. When I had finished, I stood up and went to the bedroom. The things they were discussing were hurting me. The son wanted to know whether the father was going away because of the other man, or whether I had refused to accommodate him. The father didn't want to know of the

136

other man, but whatever he told his son seemed to hurt him. It did not take five minutes before the son came to me, crying and announcing his hatred for me.

I felt so bad. The happiness I had faded away. I found myself wishing Jack would make his stand clear. Yes, I was ready to forget everything and stay with him, if he accepted it. The son meant so much to me and I hated to see his happiness disturbed, especially now that he was sitting for his CPE. That would interfere with his performance in the examinations. Furthermore I still loved Jack and there was nothing which could please me more than having him again, and with a happy son, as we had earlier longed for. But, would he forget and forgive me for the daughter I had got? Would his pride allow him to stoop that low?

"Son," I called. "Go back to your dad and tell him I want him to stay. Tell him to come with all his belongings and stay with us. Go."

He stopped crying and went to his father. I could hear them talk. Then Jack sent for me. When I got there, he sent the son away with fifty shillings. He turned to me.

"Milly, are you serious about having me back?"

It was a difficult question, which needed time to answer. But I did not give myself the time. "Yes. If you are ready to forgive me. Can't you see how much we are hurting our son? He loves you dearly," I said.

He pulled me to him and kissed me. My heartbeats were almost audible. I got hold of his waist and again pulled him to myself. I looked at his face closely and sensed something unusual. He wasn't the same man; I mean, he wasn't the same Jack I knew in the sixties. This was Jack of the eighties. He had a face that had bitterness written all over it. He was a tired Jack, who would no longer be happy. Jack who wouldn't forgive and who wouldn't forget.

137

But still looking responsible. I too sensed that he had some bad news for me and that was probably why he had sent the son out.

"Jack," I called and kissed his cheek. "Please do not hurt me. Do not tell me what you want to. I can see you have something bad in store for me, but please let it wait. It will kill me, Jack."

"No, Milly. I must tell it to you. We must talk."

"But I love you, Jack. There is no question about that and you know it. Why don't we bury the differences we have right now and start all over again?"

"I wronged you once, Milly. I do not want to repeat it."

"But I understand. I have also wronged you, dear. Can't we forget that and start becoming one from this minute onward?"

"The heart is willing, dear Milly, but the spirit is protesting. Have you ever felt like that?"

"Not where you are concerned, Jack. Please let us..."

"No, Milly. Never. I am not good for you now. Prison changed me, Milly. I want to lead a solitary life. My love was disturbed by roaring warders and uncooperative prisoners. I lose my temper easily and become violent. I do not want this to happen in your presence. Please try to understand. I have always loved you. I do not know how long it will take me to forget that you were once mine. I want to forget you, Milly. I want to forget my son as well. I will not want to see you again, because that will always remind me of you. When I go, remain with my love, give the love to your fiancé, and try to be happy. I'll be happy leading a solitary life waiting for another Milly, if there will ever be one. All I would like you to..."

"Jack, has my daughter anything to do with your decision?"

138

"God! No. I love her. You got her after nine years, which makes me love you all the more. No one can imagine a beautiful young girl like you to be faithful for so long."

I held him more tightly. I couldn't believe he was serious. But he was understanding, he wanted me to be happy, which I wasn't going to be, knowing that there would soon be someone else in his heart. Someone who would experience "true love" from a true lover. She wouldn't have to worry because it was evident that Jack had reformed. I was jealous.

"You do not want to see me again, Jack?"

"No, dear. Never!"

"What do I tell our son?"

"I do not have a son, Milly. He is your son. Make him understand that."

"But he won't. We have tried that a hundred times."

"Keep on trying. Why give up hope so early? When I keep away, he will get used to the phoney father." That was an insult which I ignored.

He pushed me away from him after kissing me. I knew what was happening in him and he did not want it to get over him. He went to the door and opened it. He looked outside, then turned to me. He stared at me as if I were a stranger to him. At last, he managed a smile. The lovely smile I once knew and admired, I felt like going to him and crushing his ribs with my hold. But I didn't move. Some instinct in me told me that it was all over. He wasn't mine, but I wanted to see him again, just like when I had first met him in school. My courage came back and I called.

"Jack...I know it is all over, but please do me a last favour."

He hesitated, the smile still calling me to him but I resisted with immeasurable effort.

"The last favour..." he repeated after me. "Mention it and let it be the last, for my sake."

"My younger sister, Mumbi, who was only five when you went to prison, will be having a pre-wedding party next Saturday. Promise me you will attend."

The smile went away. His face darkened and looked pale. The bitterness I had noticed came to life. It was evident he did not expect a request of ever meeting me again. But, he had committed himself and I knew he wouldn't back out.

"Where will that be?"

"At the Railway Club. I'll be there from 3.00 p.m. till the party is over."

"See you then," he said and left.

The sound of Tonny's Volkswagen called Zollo Junior from his bedroom, where he was doing his studies. It was 8.00 p.m. and we had had supper. Junior hated Tonny (my fiancé) and this night I knew there would be trouble between the two, especially now that Junior had met his father and was expecting him this same night.

I too didn't feel like having Tonny that night. I had much to think about Jack's reappearance in my life and I wanted to be left alone. I could also sense some quarrel between me and Junior and I was worried. He had insisted that when his dad came he should be called, no matter what time it was. He talked to me as the sound of Tonny locking his car's door reached us.

"Mum, do not open for Tonny. My dad won't be happy if he meets him here."

"I'll open for him, prepare a cup of tea for him and then ask him to go. Do not misbehave, son. Please be kind to him."

"But dad won't like it, mum. I am going to tell him..."

140

"Please, go back to your studies and leave this to me. Tonny likes you very much; why do you hate him? Please go. I'll call you when dad comes."

That made him go, but he was still unhappy.

Jack arrived at the pre-wedding party at around 8.00 p.m. I was outside the hall when the car arrived. At first I couldn't recognise the two people in it; the couple I mean. The car was parked a few metres from where I stood. A young, tall girl stepped out. She looked beautiful, which was the first thing I noticed about her. Her way of dressing was admirable and the way she had done her hair told me, without doubt, that she wasn't giving the latest fashion a chance to pass her by. Our eyes met and we seemed to like each other. She didn't wait for her companion, as he locked the offside door. She came to me. We shook hands as if we had met before, then I welcomed her into the hall. With me, she didn't have to buy a carnation, which was a requirement at the door. I decided to let her pass; her boyfriend, husband, or fiancé would pay for his. It would save him twenty shillings.

"I am Miriam Nyambiu, the eldest sister to the bride," I introduced myself, as we entered the hall.

"I am Jacqueline Mbogo. It's kind of you to show me inside. Thank you."

"Welcome. It was a plaesure to meet you."

I took her to a room where the host was entertaining his relatives and closest friends. As she met the others, I went out to meet her friend, still unsure whether Jack had arrived. It was because of him that I spent most of the evening outside the hall. I was sure he would come for he had promised to and he knew how to keep his word.

I met him at the door as he paid for a flower. I quickened

my steps and reached him before he handed over the money.

"I'll pay for you. I invited you," I called.

"Oh, hello there. I must have kept you waiting."

"Not for long. How do you do?"

"I do well. Welcome to the party."

"Thank you." He followed me. I was excited. This was the very Jack who had introduced me to the world and taken care of me when I was in school, the man who was to be my husband, a man I had sinned and got a son with. He was with me again, looking almost as young as when I had met him. He had dressed himself so impressively that walking beside him made me feel great. I was crazy about this lover boy.

"Tonight is going to be our last day meeting," I told myself. I was going to exploit every minute he was here. Dance with him throughout, get him in private and really have him; exhaust him as I have never done to anyone before, even to him. I wanted this day to be a day to remember in life. I took his hand and led him to the VIP room. As far as I was concerned, there were no more visitors coming. I wasn't going to wait outside the hall again; Jack was with me.

My fiancé Tonny had arrived early in the evening. He had stayed with us for about three hours and since he neither drank beer nor danced, he had found the place boring, and left. I had also passed word to him that I would be very much engaged and he should not expect to see much of me throughout the night. He had not argued. "This night," I had said to myself, "I am all for Jack. It is our day of saying goodbye forever." I wasn't sure of that either; it would be hard to forget a person you love.

I gave Jack a seat and then called my sister and her

142

husband-to-be. My excitement told them the man at hand was to be respected. When I mentioned his name, their mouths were wide open. Who hadn't heard about him, anyway?

I left them talking. I was sure they were not going to let him get out of their sight. They were always eager to see this man who had got me crazy; the man I had always gone to see in prison; the man I was to marry over fourteen years ago.

I passed where Jacqueline was. She was talking with another young man, but a look at her told me she wasn't enjoying it. I could see she was missing someone, the boyfriend she had come with, who up to now hadn't entered, as far as I was concerned. It was my mistake, because the man didn't know where I had taken her. So, it was my duty to trace him for her and bring him. Jacqueline was a girl whom I had liked at first sight and I wanted her to be happy. She looked like a girl who'd dance beautifully and I wanted to watch her.

"Hello, Jacqueline, I am sorry we lost your friend. I shouldn't have brought you straight in; he must be looking for you everywhere. Mind to come with me to the hall and look for him? I never saw his face so I can't know him."

Jacqueline looked confused, till I wondered why. I thought I had wronged her to have mentioned her boyfriend in the presence of the young man she was talking to. Then she seemed to get the picture. She told me:

"Thank you, Miriam, you are wonderful. You brought my man three minutes ago."

"Is it? I am not aware. The work I've done here has left me confused."

"Thanks a lot for your concern. I am talking with a 'new friend' here. He is Lawrence Wanyoike."

143

"A pleasure to meet you Lenny. I am Miriam Nyambiu."
We shook hands, then I turned to Jacqueline.
"I thought you'd introduced me to your real..."
"But I thought you knew each other. You just walked
in hand-in-hand with him. I am sorry. Excuse me Mr
Wanyoike, let me introduce my friend hereto my fiancé."
My heart was racing as she stood up. The picture now
had come clearly to my mind. But I could not believe it.
It was the truth, but I did not want to accept it. I follow-
ed her, my hand in hers as she was leading me to Jack, who
was seated, much engaged in talk with my younger sister,
Njambi and her husband-to-be, Alex Mwangi, "The man
from Illard" as we used to call him.
"Lord," I prayed, "Please do not let this happen to me.
Let this dream come to an end before I faint. Oh...Lord."
Lord heeded my short prayers, I did not collapse on my
knees, which had almost given in. I got courage and
managed to smile. The first thing I noticed when my eyes
focussed again was Jack's smile. It was different from the
one I knew; this one was the most wonderful thing I ever
saw. But it wasn't meant for me, it was meant for Jacqueline
Mbogo. All those years, it had been reserved for her. Yes!
This man was not meant for me. If he were, I'd have known
that smile. I gave up. I knew Jack had been serious when
he had said that he wanted to forget me. There was Jacqueline, young and beautiful, and kind-hearted, learning
from the few minutes I had known her. Well, I couldn't
blame him. I was 32 and about to show my age on the face.
Jacqueline was about twenty, if not younger. That made
all the difference in life, in Jack's life. I didn't know whether
to be happy or angry, but the truth was written all over
my face; I was damn jealous.
The pre-wedding lost taste, as far as I was concerned.

144

I knew Jacqueline wasn't going to give me time to take Jack aside. There wasn't any need for that anyway. Why have pride out of a borrowed dress? A dress that can be asked back any time the owner wanted it. There was only one thing to do now, to seek leave and move out of the party, to take a taxi and go back to Junior for comfort.

I excused myself, after introductions. Jacqueline followed me outside and to the hall. People were dancing in couples, most of them with bottles of beer in their hands. The whole party was wonderful; everyone was happy, except Miriam, ME.

I saw Jacqueline to the "Ladies" and waited for her. We hadn't talked much, I was afraid that if we did, I would give myself away. As we went back to the dancing hall, we met Jack. He stopped to take my hand, then he led me to the floor and we started dancing, the last dance in my life.

A borrowed dress, I thought as I saw Jacqueline coming to demand it from me in the daylight. "She's coming for you, Jack. She's a nice girl. When are you marrying her?"

"She's my wife, I am staying with her. But if you mean a wedding, that will never happen in my life. I guess you know why."

"Who is she?"

"She is my wife. My own."

"I have heard that. I mean what does she do?" I sounded annoyed.

"Exactly what she is supposed to do. To serve me as her only husband." I knew he had understood what I wanted to know but was only giving me a hard time.

"Where is she working? Is it bad to ask? Does it hurt you?"

"Three questions at a go. You are curious. It doesn't hurt

145

me, and it is not bad to ask. Milly, there is one thing we are omitting in Jacqueline's name, otherwise you would not have asked. She's Doctor Mbogo." He spoke with a touch of pride.

But, Jesus! A doctor at her age! Anyway, who had told me her age, but myself. She reached where we had stopped, dancing but going round on the same spot to give ourselves time to talk.

"I am a jealous, Lady Miriam. Just excuse me. This husband of mine is very slippery. He hardly gets out of my sight. I wouldn't allow that, every lady I meet seems to have a go at him. Can't allow it."

"Jesus!" I thought loudly. "What a bad thing to tell me? She shouldn't have told me that. Why? She should know I was the first woman in his life. Does she think at his age he hasn't had other women? Doesn't that show how little she knows about Jack? I'll let her know, I'll make her understand she shouldn't go out talking like that, despite what she is. A doctor or not, she amounts to the same thing; a wife of a man just like any of us." I knew she didn't mean to be rude: she was only humorous but my jealousy had outdone me.

I just stood there, undecided on whether to carry on or to let her know that Jack was mine for the past decade and a half, up to this moment when they were dancing.

They passed near without looking at me. Jacqueline's head was resting on his shoulder and she was bending a little, because he was slightly shorter. Her breasts were squeezed against his chest as they danced a slow waltz. They didn't seem to notice me, though I was sure that they were aware of my presence.

Jack had left me; the dance I had with him was a sign of "Goodbye". I wished he had not reappeared in my life,

146

which would no longer be the same again. "A life with a criminal," I thought, "is wonderful but short-lived."

Junior! Oh my Junior! Where are you? Come and give me comfort. I started off for the door. You'd think I had realized I was stepping on a rattlesnake. At the door I stopped to look behind; I wanted to make sure I wasn't dreaming, that Jack was in the hall, dancing with a lady he called his wife. Yes! it was true, it was Jack, the Jack of the eighties and not sixties; a reformed Jack, as the word went. Our eyes met. I thought I saw him wink to rebuke me. Then he raised up his right hand and started waving me goodbye. Jacqueline noticed what was going on and turned. She smiled and waved her hand too. I looked at them waving; they looked the best couple in the hall, but to me, the worst, yes — even foolish. Why rebuke me? I turned and left. A taxi had just brought another couple. It was nearing 10.00 p.m. As far as I was concerned, the party was no more. But there was Junior for me, ever for me. Why not go back to him and feel Jack's presence as I used to all the time he was in prison?

The uncouth, ruthless, irresponsible and stupid Jack Zollo. Who does he think he is? Isn't he, after all, a criminal? Who can reform that bastard, anyway? The man-eater. To hell with him!

But did all my insults amount to anything? They were unjust and I knew it. They wouldn't help me; they couldn't make me forget the real good man he was. The truth of what he had said dawned on me. Indeed, anyone thinking of the future is a dreamer. I was a dreamer: I had put too much attention on my future and ended up weeping myself dry. Look at Jack, who has never wasted time thinking of the future, and see how happy he is now; his memories of the rotten past buried deep in the ocean. "Jacqueline," I said as I got into the taxi, "I envy you, but you are a nice girl. No doubt about that; you are lucky and you'll soon know. God bless the two of you. As for me, I have Junior to think about."

I hailed the taxi as it made to take off. Forty shillings was all I needed to reach home. Goodbye, Jack Zollo.